THE CURE, THE KILLER, AND RUSS BURTON

JAKE CAYMAN

ISBN-13: 979-8-9985925-1-5

To Lady L.

THE CURE

THE KILLER

AND RUSS BURTON

JAKE CAYMAN

PROLOGUE
Russ Burton
My Journaling App
Entry #97

It's not the stars that fascinate me. It's the space between them. The darkness. But right now, I'm wasting time. I need to focus. Two days until graduation, and my speech isn't even finished. Two days! Why did I get myself into this?

1

The microphone sucks the air from Russ Burton's chest. His lungs, though healthy and pink, all but stop functioning. He can't swallow, his tongue and throat too dry, his mouth rough and scratchy like the hotel towels from last night's pre-graduation party.

Russ's skin begins to lose color, beige cheeks turning whitish gray. His brain, though capable, rings like an alarm, warning of pending humiliation, pleading for him to flee but knowing he can't.

Perhaps it's the five thousand eyeballs staring at him that retriggers his respiratory system. His tightened chest expands. But his stomach is overwhelmed, on the verge of vomiting. His legs shake, and the pole-style podium offers no place to hide them.

In the record-breaking June heat, the onlookers fan their primped faces with event programs. The graduates, fidgeting in white fold-out chairs lined across the field, chitchat and smile and wave at family in the stands who enthusiastically wave back, yelling, "We love you, Sofia!" (or John, or Katelyn, or whoever).

Russ winces at the words on his tablet, second-guessing the lines in his speech attacking the principal, Dr. Marvin Eckspun, better known to students as Dr. Explosion for his hot-tempered overreactions on disciplinary matters—a man wanting for the days of corporal punishment, when he could paddle troublemakers in front of the class.

Russ's thoughts pinball: *Just skip it*; *Do it*; *You're the valedictorian, don't*; *But . . . Explosion deserves it.* His internal deliberation ceases when Dr. Eckspun, sitting to Russ's immediate right, the first in a line of administrators and teachers in green-and-black academic regalia, taps his cane and coughs an *ahem* so loudly the phony throat-clearing permeates the microphone and broadcasts out through the concert-style speakers at the front of the stage. Mild laughter ensues from the crowd.

In a final awkward hesitation, Russ grabs the plastic water bottle he'd placed at his feet. The restless onlookers wait as he cracks the cap, takes a sip, and sets it back down. Russ brushes the dangling gold tassel off his unshaven but hairless face and meets the swarm of eyeballs again. He spots Tara Saay in the bleachers, a senior whom Dr. Eckspun banned from walking in the ceremony three days earlier. Russ finds her easily—Tara's bright white halter top and black choker, with a skull medallion, stand out. She is next to her mother, who sits erect, as always, wearing scores of jewels on her neck and wrists. Russ shies away, looking down at his tablet, unable as always to meet Tara's eyes.

Her flight to California—for UCLA—leaves in the morning. There was no sense in delaying it, she told Russ, now that Explosion had ruined her. Russ agreed: the faster she could get out of this hellhole, the better. But since then, Russ has endured the image of her plane taking off replaying in his mind, filling him with dread, sick at the idea he'll see her only on her social media, which he already frequents daily. Multiple times daily.

"My fellow . . ." Russ says before starting over. "My fellow graduates."

Chitter-chatter continues in the crowd.

"As we come to the end of our four-year journey, we take this moment to reflect on what we've learned and to give thanks to all those who've helped us along the way. They deserve so much credit."

His mother is first on the list, but not because she deserves it. She isn't even there. All flights have been cancelled out of Cancun, she told him, and she's devastated—apparently—that she won't be able to make it. Hopefully, she said, she could livestream it. But Russ knows she won't. He also knows direct flights to Seattle were available. Going on vacation the week of graduation was ridiculous in the first place. Just like her.

"I wouldn't be here today without my mom." Russ presses his fist against his lip.

The crowd hushes.

"She's been there each step of the way, guiding me, encouraging me." He hurries to the next line. "You all have people to thank too, so let me pause so you can let them hear it."

Graduates leap up, blowing kisses, covering their hearts and pointing at family.

As they settle down, Russ continues.

"I'd like to thank all of you, my classmates, for making our journey unforgettable . . ."

Truthfully, Russ would love to forget most of these fools.

"It's been a hell of a ride at North Seattle High."

Hoots and hollers spring from the crowd.

"We've learned so much, from so many. Mr. Huang, our humanities teacher, instilled in us the importance of history and the significance of the stories people leave behind for future generations."

An airliner screams overhead. Russ waits.

"Stone tablets were one of the first ways people recorded stories."

Russ raises his iPad.

"Make your story a memorable one. People will one day look at this tablet the same way we look at a stone one now."

The crowd gives more eye rolls than laughs.

Russ swipes up on the screen.

"Hopefully, during the last four years, you've found a purpose, or at least a pursuit. I found mine recently: finance. Sounds boring. But think *Wolf of Wall Street*, without prison. I'll let you know when we're up and running."

Eckspun shakes his head.

"Some of you are off to be athletes, like my friend Will Bayman. A guy who never played organized sports but who walked onto the football team three years ago and has been killing quarterbacks ever since."

The graduates erupt into cheers and chants of "Wil-lee B, Wil-lee B."

"And he'll continue the slaughter over at Eastern Washington University."

The chants for Will get louder. With his six-foot-five frame and Nordic-descent blond hair, Will stands up from in the center of his classmates. He smiles, revealing two rows of white teeth solid as dice and dimples big enough to fit diamonds. He takes a bow and points at Russ as if to say, *My man*.

Before Dr. Eckspun reacts, Ms. Trexel, an English teacher not far removed from her own college graduation, stands and motions for Will to sit. Will tilts his head and gives her a little finger wave, instigating multiple cat-call-whistles from male graduates who barely passed her classes, distracted by her trendy, tight-fitting sweaters. Will sits, and the crowd settles again.

Eckspun glares at Russ, his gray brow furrowed, coarse as porcupine quills.

Russ checks the next line. This is it. Attack or retreat.

He finds Tara's eyes. She nods.

Attack.

"Some of you are going into the arts."

Tara leans forward, propping her elbow on her sun-browned thigh, setting her chin in her hand, three rings pressing into her cheek. Her mother folds her arms.

"One of our standout artists is a student who has generously shared her art around this school, her murals bringing life to these walls."

Eckspun angles himself toward the podium. Ms. Trexel's eyes widen, and she shakes her head at Russ. Please, no.

Russ carries on.

"Tara's latest masterpiece, sadly, was painted over just three days ago. It was a sight to see, created under the streetlamps in just one night. The next morning, the rising sun revealed a breathtaking scene on the administration building, at the front of the school: a student, slumped forward in his chair, a shadowy figure behind him shaking their fist."

Dr. Eckspun pounds the side of his seat. Ms. Trexel shudders and gives him a shocked look.

"Even though she's painted three other murals around this school, this one was deemed vandalism, not art. Now, in all fairness, this one perhaps was completed without permission and—unlike the other murals—did not have a hefty donation attached from the Saay family."

Tara's mother grins, as if amused, and nods in agreement.

Eckspun launches out of his seat, rising above Russ, extending his alien-long fingers around the microphone, his palm covering the microphone's head. A muffled sound rips through the speakers. His white mustache pokes the rim of Russ's ear. "Knock it the hell off and act like a goddamn valedictorian."

Russ freezes.

The students begin booing, and Dr. Eckspun snaps his hand off the microphone, his face red and wrinkled like a demon's as he returns to his seat.

"It's okay," Russ says. "Take a seat, please." He grabs his water, doing his best to keep it steady as he sips.

Someone yells from the crowd: "Dr. Explosion sucks!" More boos rain down before all the students take their seats again.

Russ could move to wrap up the speech now, and have a victory, but he doesn't.

"There's one last person we need to talk about, a person who knows the stories of this place better than anyone. He spent twenty-five years wheeling garbage cans over sidewalk grooves—*kerchunk, kerchunk*—each one a tick closer to retirement. Though he was much older, he was one of us, a voluntary participant here, but trapped in a way. And since he officially retired yesterday, after months of fighting with the retirement board, I'd like to thank the best janitor of all time, the GOAT: Mr. J-Jack."

One student stands and makes a mopping motion as a tribute, but it doesn't catch on. A classmate pulls him down into his seat.

"He was a guide and a protector, watching out for us. He was the equalizer, someone in the circle of power—the adults in charge—who could even the playing field. Though I'll refrain from giving details, many unwarranted disciplinary acts were prevented by his interference."

Russ licks his lips, readying his mouth for the words to come.

"J-Jack overheard a lot in his time here. And he knew the drama on both sides—teachers and students alike."

Eckspun starts to get up, but Ms. Trexel pats his leg. "Just let him finish," she whispers, but loud enough for Russ to hear, "it's not worth it." He settles back.

"Believe it or not, things were a lot different here thirty years ago: this place was a little more *Wolf of Wall Street* than you might think. Not the finance stuff, but the parties. Wild, freaky parties in the administration building.

Organized by the best rule man this place has ever seen: Dr. Eckspun. There are pictures to prove—"

Before the crowd can process this, Eckspun grabs the back of Russ's neck, cinching with his bony fingers like pliers, squeezing on two pressure points. He forces Russ onto all fours. Russ drops the tablet, sending it tumbling across the stage.

"Get off me!" Russ screams.

Eckspun raises his cane. "Disgracing this school won't be tolerated," he yells, swatting down on Russ's backside.

Russ yelps like a puppy, thrashing about, unable to break away.

The crowd gasps.

With Russ on his stomach, rolling from side to side, Explosion readies the cane for a second swat. As he strikes down, Ms. Trexel dives on the old man, sending him flying sideways, his head slamming onto the stage, stunning him. Russ scurries to his feet, tripping on his gown, stumbling but catching his balance. He meets the five thousand eyeballs once again—along with all the phones pointing at him.

2

The common understanding of fight-or-flight—the automatic reactions of animals to stressful situations—often fails to acknowledge the third option: to freeze, to do nothing, to hope it all works out, like a deer in a hunter's spotlight. Like Russ Burton now, just standing there at the front of the stage, confused, undecisive, with hundreds of phones recording him. The crowd is in shock, their eyes wide, some spectators covering their mouths or whispering to each other.

Next to Russ, the podium lies overturned. Next to the microphone, Ms. Trexel looms over Dr. Eckspun, smoothing her gown, demanding he not move until help arrives. Yoga and weight training six days weekly has paid off: Ms. Trexel just leveled a man nearly twice her size, a man who now lies there discombobulated, blood oozing from his brow, down his cheek, soaking into his white mustache, turning it pink. He is dazed and likely concussed, and in his confusion seems more than willing to stay put. Around the stage, teachers and administrators move about, having abandoned their orderly line of chairs. Most staff mill aimlessly, but a few are talking on their cell phones, probably calling the authorities.

The spectators stay in the crowd—except for the largest graduate, Will Bayman, who is charging at the stage, charging along the same field where he's been killing quarterbacks for the last three years, as Russ mentioned in his speech. Despite his massive frame, Will jumps onto the five-foot-high stage with ease, like a kid hopping up onto a curb. He snatches up the podium at its pole. Feedback screeches out of the speakers. Holding the podium in the air, the square base hovering above his knees, Will brings the microphone to his lips, pausing until the crowd noise dwindles. "This is how we do!" Will yells, with the energy of a pro wrestler on cable TV. "North Seattle High, can you hear me!"

Some scattered cheers.

"I said . . . NSH, can you hear me!"

Now the graduates roar.

Russ begins to unfreeze. Turning sideways to face Will, Russ makes the crowd and their cameras either settle for his profile or pan over to the new star of the show. As he keeps his eyes on his friend marching along the front of the stage like the leader of a pep rally, Russ tries to process what just happened, the gravity of the situation settling in his gut like a sharp rock.

Will's size-fourteen loafers step inches from Eckspun's head. "Finally, someone had the balls to serve one up to Dr. Explosion," he says, glaring down at the old man.

Eckspun sits up, groaning. Ms. Trexel kneels, placing her hand on his back. "Lie back down until help gets here," she says, before turning her attention to Will. "Will, put down the mic, please."

Will either doesn't hear or doesn't listen.

"Give it up for our valedictorian," Will says, wrapping his muscle-packed arm around Russ's shoulders. "You all just witnessed the greatest speech in NSH *history*." As cheers follow, Will reaches down behind Russ and slaps him on the butt, like football players do. Russ flinches. "Oops, sorry bro." He places his arm back around Russ. "It probably still stings."

The crowd laughs. Russ chuckles too, but the word "history" lingers in his mind. His public spanking is now part of recorded history, and he'll forever be the guy who got spanked by an old man—and not just in front of everyone here, but everyone who would see it online. Forever.

A woman, who is nearly as short as she is wide, walks out from the wandering teachers at the back of the stage and approaches the two instigators. Although they aren't related, Will and Russ look like they could be brothers, but Russ would be the runt of the litter—a head shorter, much thinner, and with darker hair. "Mr. Bayman," she says sternly, "you need to return to your seat."

Her name: Assistant Vice Principal Molbeck. Her nickname: Ms. Mole-Big. The reason is obvious—a prune-sized mole that lives in the crease between her chin and her double-chin, poking out and retreating with each change in facial expression. She's had the mole removed twice, but it comes back stronger and longer each time. "Now!" she orders, gripping and pulling the pole. "Let. Go."

Will holds it for a second longer, then releases, sending Ms. Mole-Big stumbling back, tripping over Dr. Eckspun, thudding down on her fat rump. She struggles to rise, having to roll over onto her couch-cushion-belly, a position where she can get to her knees.

As she struggles up, Mr. Ziegler, a math teacher and tennis coach, a man with strands of hair spiraled on the back of his head, points at Will. "You need to exit this stage, Mr. Bayman." Like the growl of a pit bull, his tone is low and serious, perhaps spurred from fear of incitement, fear that Will could start a riot, or perhaps Mr. Ziegler still has feelings for Ms. Mole-Big, whom he used to accompany to those parties Russ mentioned.

"No problem, Coach," Will says. He pats Russ on the rear, lighter this time, and hops off the stage.

Ms. Molbeck stands and readies the podium at her front. "Please remain in your seats," she says. "Once law enforcement arrives and addresses the situation, we will continue the ceremony."

As Ms. Mole-Big goes on, thanking everyone for their patience, Mr. Huang whispers to Russ, telling him to follow. They exit down the side stairs and disappear behind the stage, completely out of sight once beyond the gymnasium. The crowd noise dissipates.

Mr. Huang walks with his hands behind his back, the knuckles of one hand in the other's palm. His legs glide under his gown, his knees never seeming to touch the fabric, creating the illusion that he's floating. Although Mr. Huang's gown has the same base colors as the other faculty's, green and black, his sleeves have three white stripes, signifying his doctorate in humanities.

"Are we going to the office?" Russ asks.

"Is that where you'd like to go?"

Russ shrugs.

"I'm not sure I've seen a spectacle so odd." Mr. Huang pauses. He's a notorious pauser, constantly breaking between sentences as if the listener needs extra time to absorb the idea. "It's unnerving the way people act, so out of character, when the slightest social rule is broken."

Russ isn't sure if he's talking about him, Dr. Eckspun, Ms. Trexel, Will, Ms. Molbeck, or the whole lot.

As they pass the office and enter the parking lot, it's clear they're heading for Mr. Huang's classroom. It's a portable, a faded modular building with taupe paint that's peeling in streaks, located at the back corner of the lot, where a dozen parking spaces were sacrificed for its placement.

Once inside, in the stillness of the classroom, Russ realizes he's shaking, his insides rattling. To keep his balance, he posts against the counter along the far wall where Mr. Huang, during class, would set out copies of ancient texts, Renaissance art, and replica artifacts. Russ and Will would join there for group work, pretending to admire the displays but mostly making plans extracurricular in nature.

Russ was not a naturally gifted student, so becoming valedictorian required extra work, which he preferred to do when no one was looking. Although he lacked giftedness, he had fear—fear of being average and disappointing. Additionally, he had the ability to go with little sleep, allowing him to study and work into the early-morning hours. Moreover, he examined and understood the intricate details of the school's selection rules, a suggestion from J-Jack, positioning himself with the best claim to the title.

The blinds are metal and gray. Mr. Huang lifts a slat. Light slices through the opening, dust swirling in it. "The police have arrived," he says, "up at the office. It's probably best you talk to them down here. There are many spies looking through cameras in administration."

This classroom, a giant box filled with empty desks, where each school day Russ joined thirty other kids, concentrating on Mr. Huang's lecture—or at least appearing to—seems foreign now. Today, it's basically empty and lifeless. There are no good distractions, no kids goofing or talking shit, and Russ uncontrollably reflects on the ceremony, the spanking, the chaos. His involuntary rumination stretches from his mind to his gut. He winces, his stomach tightening. He's shaken, and the vomiting feeling is right below his throat. He begins to doubt he made the right move, going after Eckspun. It sure wasn't worth a public lashing. The caning—the spanking—will be what everyone, including Tara, will remember.

Mr. Huang sits against the edge of his desk. It's always clean; there's nothing on it but a legal pad framed in the upper right corner, ready for good ideas. "Russ, I'll bring the police down here for you," he says. "When they get here, you can ask them for a representative. I will be that for you, should you please."

Russ sidesteps to a waste basket halfway to the wall, ready to snatch it if he pukes. "Like as a lawyer? Why? It's not like they can arrest me."

Mr. Huang nods in agreement. "Yes, as your lawyer. I do have a bar card. Law school preceded my pursuit of humanities. And, yes, you probably did nothing illegal."

Russ leans off the counter. "Probably?"

"Well, if the police can find the right penal code, having just the right legal language, and a few convenient investigatory details, they could charge anyone with something, they could charge you with . . . incitement, for example. Maybe it is nothing to worry about, but Dr. Eckspun has a host of friends, including most of City Hall. He won't get out of this though, impossible. He is done. Should he refuse to retire, the Board will have to fire him. And he will be charged, with something anyway, but that doesn't mean his friends won't try something, especially if they themselves have exposure regarding those pictures you spoke of."

Russ chokes down vomit.

"Take a breath," Mr. Huang says, removing his cap and gown. "I'm going up to the office. I'll tell them you are secured in my classroom." He folds the gown on the desk, squares it next to the legal pad, and sets his cap on top. "When we arrive back here, you should ask for someone to be present, even if you prefer that be someone other than myself."

Russ nods, afraid he'll barf if he talks.

Mr. Huang stands in the doorway. "Russ, in case I don't get a chance to tell you later, I know you will do something important with your life." He starts out the door but pauses and turns back. "And I don't mean being some rowdy and fancy stockbroker."

Mr. Huang shuts the door and is gone.

Russ kneels over the waste basket and vomits. One long, emptying barf, no dry heaving or gagging. As he backs away and finds his breath, his stomach settles. He slips his gown off over his head, careful not to smear puke-splatters onto his clothes. Russ drops the poofy wad of polyester into the waste basket. It slides down the black plastic liner, wiping the sides, covering the pile at the bottom.

Cool air soaks into Russ's damp, classic white, slim-fit, spread-collar dress shirt, which he selected three days ago at Kohl's only after trying on nine other shirts. Exiting the dressing room, he left behind a mound of clothes on the floor and shirt pins piled on the bench—not realizing the magnet strip on the wall was a pin-holder.

Russ peeks out the blinds. Up at the office, Mr. Huang is talking to two cops. He breaks into a cold sweat, not sure if it's from throwing up or because he wants nothing to do with talking to the police. What's the point? Like Mr. Huang said, Eckspun can't get out of this. So why should Russ risk saying anything damning? Besides, he doesn't want Will to think he's already left. Russ cracks the door and looks around. He slips out, leaving the puke-filled waste basket behind. At least J-Jack won't have to clean it.

With quick, light steps down the ramp, Russ stays low and out of sight, scampering to Will's metallic-gray Chevy Silverado at the opposite corner. Will drove Russ to the ceremony, backing his truck into the same spot as always: the dirt shoulder next to the last parking space.

Russ tries the door handles, but they're locked, of course. He checks that no one is watching, then climbs into the truck bed and lies on the bed liner, concealing himself behind the side walls. He pulls his phone from the pocket of his slacks. In the distance, music plays: the graduation song, Pomp and Circumstance. They've gone on without him, their valedictorian.

Russ hesitates before waking his phone. When he does, seven notifications appear. He swipes through them. They're all about the spanking. Texts and posts: peach and clap emojis, *nice speech red cheeks*, shocked face emoji, *way to take one for the team*, rolling-on-the-floor-laughing emoji. Worst of all, there are videos. As the first one loads, his body goes numb.

Seeing the stage from a spectator's view is surreal. The clip could easily be a viral video, the ones nobody really thinks could happen to them, the ones that always—because they're so bizarre—receive a slew of comments about the video being fake. But this did happen. And there he is: Russ Burton, valedictorian, provoking an old man, the old man pinning the provoker, striking with his old-man cane, the impact like the snap of a two-by-four. The worst part? The yelp. How weak and helpless.

Russ wants to melt into the bed of the truck. But he keeps watching: Ms. Trexel clobbering Explosion, Will taking the mic, directing attention off Russ, Ms. Molbeck butting in and falling over, Mr. Huang guiding Russ away, paramedics and police arriving, examining Eckspun, and finally the officers escorting him offstage.

The numbness in Russ's body turns sharp, like icepicks jabbing his skin. Russ rolls to his side, bringing his knees to his elbows, positioned like a full-term fetus. His identity has changed: he'll forever be the valedictorian—no, the boy—who was lashed, spanked publicly at graduation. What a mistake. He should have never provoked Eckspun like that. Sure, Explosion is finished, but now the person Russ used to be is dead, replaced by someone worse, someone who definitely has no chance with Tara, not that his chances have ever been great.

Russ texts his mom:

Can you talk?
No.
Graduation didn't go good.
I already heard. Unbelievable. You couldn't just act like a valedictorian.

Russ swallows hard. His thumbs hover over the screen, ready to type, *I'm sorry*. But he clicks off his phone instead.

In the distance, the crowd cheers, probably the graduates tossing their caps. Soon, they'll fill the parking lot: excited, stunned new adults, racing to their cars, the starting line of their new lives. They'll leave with an unbelievable graduation story. A story they'll tell for years, decades even, pulling up the video with a simple search: *spanking at North*—the search engine populating the rest—*Seattle High.*

Will is the first graduate to the parking lot. Jogging to his truck, he's still in his gown, the cap under his arm, two rolled-up pieces of paper tied with red bows inserted over two of his fingers.

"Where the hell is he?" Will mutters, approaching the truck, slowing to a walk.

"In here," Russ whispers.

Will leans over the side wall. "What the hell, bro?"

"I'm laying low."

"You that embarrassed?" Will lowers his voice. "Get the hell out of there."

Russ peeks over the bed at Mr. Huang's classroom at the far end of the lot. "The cops are down there."

"Yeah," Will says, looking over his shoulder. "So what?"

"Huang says they could charge me with incitement or something."

"What? No way. They can't arrest you. That's crazy."

"He says Eckspun has connections."

Will shakes his head. "Bro, they got Explosion in cuffs right now. He's done. You got him. There is no way in hell they can charge you."

"Well, I'd rather not find out."

Part of that is true, but mostly Russ really doesn't want to be seen by anyone.

Graduates start filling the parking lot. Will grins and waves to one of them as she skips along rows of cars, bouncing like a six-year-old. "Here, take this," he says, handing Russ one of the rolled-up papers, "a fake diploma for you. I can't believe they just went on with the ceremony. That was some crazy shit."

"Thanks. I'm sure my mom will cherish this."

"The real ones will be mailed, they said."

Russ fingers the ends and twirls the roll. "Maybe Tara should have it. She didn't get one."

"Bro, forget Tara."

Russ rubs his temples. "What did she say about the speech?"

"I didn't even talk to her."

Russ sighs.

"You can ask her herself at Rando's tonight. Let's get the hell out of here. For good." Will opens the rear doors to the crew cab. "Jump in here—it's tinted dark as hell, ain't nobody gonna see you."

3

Graduates hang out car windows, cheering, music thumping and horns blaring. Their vehicles swarm the exit, bottlenecking at the discharge. At the same time, more of the crowd from the ceremony descends onto the parking lot, high-fiving drivers and passengers, all optimistic and downright elated.

Will's Chevy idles at the back of the bottleneck. In the crew cab, Russ sits as low as possible, trying to avoid detection—by cops, kind of, but more so by his former classmates, who would love to make every spank joke possible, derogate him, and serve up another public embarrassment.

Will's arm is cocked out the driver's-side window. More than one girl touches it as they walk past, offering congratulations and good luck, their fingers sliding off his skin, their eyes keeping his for a few seconds as they walk by.

The graduates just can't believe it: high school is actually over, their real lives start now, and Russ Burton just got spanked in front of thousands. Listening to everyone chattering as they pass, Russ cringes. They give props to Ms. Trexel and to Will but say nothing of Russ's speech, him challenging Dr. Eckspun, him defending Tara.

Will inches the truck forward as the salutatorian, Sandra Berks, smiles, her shiny legs gliding past, her gown fitting like a dress, the hem set perfectly above her bare calves, hardened by white high heels. *Bang.* Will slams the brakes. To his front, a black-haired graduate in a flannel shirt, with Western-style snaps down the center, stands straight, his scarred hand flat on the hood, his eyes behind dark shades.

"Shit, Logan," Will says, "you alright?"

Logan Price is friends with most but real friends with no one. Unlike other people, he has no desire to fit in, wearing jeans over cowboy boots every day, even a cowboy hat sometimes, a unique look for a kid at a city school.

He bangs the hood again. "You better pay attention, Bayman," he says in his raspy voice, then strolls to the driver's side, grinning.

"I was paying attention. Just to the wrong thing." Will offers his fist.

Logan gives a fist bump. "You almost killed me."

"Please, bruh, I was barely rolling. Be mad at Sandra. She shouldn't be distracting drivers like that."

Logan rests his elbow on the driver's-side mirror and tips his glasses.

Russ stays still, hidden out of view but able to partially see.

"I know," Logan says, "she had me walking through traffic without looking both ways."

Will laughs and smacks the steering wheel, vibrating the steering column. His strength comes from a combination of great genes and weight training. Logan, on the other hand, though slender, has strength built on hard labor.

"By the way, what a speech," Logan says.

The car in front pulls a few feet forward.

"Yeah," Will says, shifting into gear. "Russ took out Explosion."

Logan steps back and walks with the truck as Will closes the gap. "From where I was sitting, it looked like Explosion took out Russ." He spits chew on the pavement.

Russ remains motionless, his stomach turning.

"Eckspun is done," Will says. "They had him in front of the office handcuffed. He's cooked."

Logan laughs with his mouth closed, then spits again. "Hey, you going to Rando's?"

"Hell yes. Last one, bruh. Let's go."

Logan nods. "What about after?"

Will checks traffic. No movement. "After? Hopefully, Sandra I guess."

Logan grins. "She still with Josh?"

"What do I care?"

Russ pictures Will flirting with Sandra while he tries not to make Tara cringe.

"Right," Logan says, "well, I think the team is meeting up."

"For what?"

"A last hurrah, I guess." Logan adds another spit to the saliva puddle next to Will's tire. "You hear about Gia?"

Traffic moves a foot. Will closes the gap, and Logan follows.

Will doesn't answer immediately. "Yeah, I heard."

This could get serious, Russ thinks. The traffic needs to move.

Logan studies Will's face. "A medical release? She's got five years left on her already lenient sentence. How's that right?"

"It's not," Will says.

"You gonna see her?"

Will tilts his head, holding Logan's stare. "You know I've got nothing to do with her anymore. Why are you asking me that?" Russ can see him clench his jaw.

Will doesn't like to talk about Gia, so most of what Russ knows of her, he knows from the internet. Search Gia Navarro and what comes up are endless hits for the Porta-Potty Pusher, charged with manslaughter at sixteen years old, charged as an adult. She entered a guilty plea and was sentenced at seventeen, serving one year in juvie before being transferred to the state penitentiary—and she was Will Bayman's ex-girlfriend.

"Yeah, well," Logan says, "sometimes we hide things, if you know what I mean."

Logan seems to look at the crew cab.

Russ holds his breath.

"No, I don't," Will says.

The line of cars out front start to pull away.

"Sure," Logan says, backing up. "Relax, bruh, I'm just fucking with you."

Someone honks from behind the truck.

Logan turns and walks away, flipping off the beeper.

Will hits the gas.

With time to kill before the party, Will drives into a wooded park on the Puget Sound, the massive waterway extending off the Pacific and into the shoreline, forking in every direction. Dust puffs up from the Chevy's knobby tires, rolling over the dirt-coated pavement. There are no clouds above the Sound. The entire Northwest is in a heatwave, the sun baking everything.

This chill spot, dubbed the Coop—as in chicken coop, as in where to bring chicks—has been a go-to for Will and

Russ and up to four dozen other NSH students for the last two years. It's empty now, but Fridays after school, or even earlier on ditch days, students packed the park.

Will gets out of the truck and stretches his arms, reaching high above the cab. Groaning like a giant, he elongates the bulging muscles in his shoulders and scapula, likely sore from yesterday's barbell shoulder presses, battle ropes, and handstand pushups. Russ hops out of the crew cab, his dress shoes landing in a wash of sand.

After grabbing a bottle from under his seat, Will strolls toward the beach. Russ follows. Beyond the tree line, there's a picnic bench, just a rock's throw from the water's edge. Silent, they move toward the bench, the bottle of Jägermeister swinging in Will's hand, half-full, the alcohol sloshing inside the glass like the Sound's water lapping ashore.

On the beach, driftwood lies scattered, white and dry and dead. Will stops next to the picnic bench, uncaps the bottle, and takes a long pull. His face is expressionless, as if he just guzzled water. After Will passes the bottle, Russ takes a swig, the total fluid ounces entering his mouth equating to about half a shot, if that. He wipes the back of his arm across his lips and returns the booze.

Raising the Jäeger in a salute, Will says, "To the Coop." He takes another long pull.

Russ waits for the bottle and raises it in turn. "To the Coop." As he tilts the Jäeger to his mouth, his lips tighten, constricting the flow of bittersweet liquor. He consumes enough, however, that the intense sweet burn sliding down his chest distracts his thoughts from his public spanking. But only for a moment.

Will sits on the tabletop and smiles. "You remember the farmers market?" he asks, leaning forward, his pipes-for-forearms resting on his thighs.

Russ posts up at the side of the table, his hip bracing against the weathered planks. "No one could forget that party." He slides his hands into his pockets. "Crops for tops—that was crazy—chicks wearing bell peppers and cantaloupes like bikinis. Best night ever."

Will shakes his head. "Of course you bring up Ms. Cantaloupes."

"Hey, Tara looked good."

Russ rethinks his description immediately. Tara looking good was an understatement. She always looked good, but that night, at the farmers market, it was too much to take. Russ could barely look without losing his breath.

Will sits upright. "I'll remind you who won the top prize—"

"I know, I know . . . Avocado Girl."

He laughs. "It was healthy eating that night, bro."

It had happened at the end of the summer before senior year, the first and only farmers market of its kind. Iconic. It was also the first party Russ attended after moving back to Seattle following two years of hell, living in Texas. Will had dragged him to the party despite his protests, but by the end, or even by the beginning, Russ was glad his friend had made him go.

Not long before the party, Russ had just become Will's tutor. Not by choice, however—Russ's mother demanded it. Funny, though, Russ learned much more from Will that summer than Will ever learned from him as a tutor. More importantly, Russ stopped thinking about Texas so much. Perhaps that was what his mom intended.

"What time does Rando's start?" Russ asks.

Will slides off the tabletop and steps onto the beach. "Whenever," he says, then hocks a loogie into the water.

Russ hangs his head. "I don't know if I'll be able to make it."

Will twists around. "Stop playing. This is our last night—"

"My mom's flying in, I think. And she's pissed."

"So what? She's always pissed."

"The graduation thing—it's different."

"No kidding it's different. It's all over the internet."

Russ rubs his temple.

"Don't give me that stuff about your mom," Will says, turning his back to Russ for a moment. A twig floats down the water. "I mean, come on, you need to show up, get it over with, act like what happened was nothing, like you won, like you got what you wanted. You goaded Eckspun into it, right? And let it happen, just so Eckspun would go down. Victory."

Russ sighs. "Yeah, maybe."

"What's the worst that could happen? You might be the butt of some jokes . . . big deal."

Russ rolls his eyes at the pun and grins.

"Don't even tell me you're tripping on Tara."

Scoffing, Russ grabs the Jäeger off the table.

"Bro, forget her."

Russ takes a full shot. Recoiling from the alcohol, he says, "It's not about Tara."

"You know what," Will says, walking back to the picnic bench, sitting, and planting his knobby elbows on the wood planking, "you need to give her some I-don't-give-a-fucks. Show her you don't care what she thinks."

Russ takes another respectable gulp off the bottle. "It's . . . whatever."

"She's not some angel, you know."

"*Angel*?" Russ leans off the table, a pinched expression on his face. Of course she's not . . . perfect. Who the hell *is*? She likes to have fun, like anyone else.

Will shakes his head, stands, and takes the Jäeger. "Just forget I said anything. Let's just go."

"Woah, wait a minute, we just got here," Russ says, raising an eyebrow. "What's up?"

"If you don't want to go to the party," Will says, standing and stretching, "then forget it."

Russ folds his long arms, tucking his fingers under his biceps, bulging his lean pair of proverbial guns, which have never fired a punch at anyone. "You're pissed I'm not going to Rando's for the fiftieth time?"

"Look," Will says, propping his black leather loafers up on the bowed bench. The worn planks sag in the middle. He leans his V-shaped torso over his leg. "It's our last one. The last party."

"You'll be four hours away at Eastern—it's not like we won't party anymore."

Will hangs his head.

"And what's your deal with Tara?" Russ asks, waiting for some type of admission.

"Tara? Like I said, forget her. You'll see. Tara cares about Tara, that's it."

Russ pinches the bottle cap lying on the table, preparing to close the Jäeger bottle.

Will sighs. "I'm not going to Eastern."

"What?"

"I withdrew my acceptance."

Russ waits for a smile, or some other indication Will is joking. It doesn't come. "Actually?"

Reluctantly, Will nods, staring down beneath the table. In the sand, a black ant crawls on a hardened French fry.

"What the hell are you talking about? You've got a scholarship. Why would you—"

"You heard Logan, right?"

Russ pauses. "About my speech?"

"No, about Gia getting out."

Anytime Russ hears Gia's name, he thinks of a por-ta-potty. More specifically, he pictures the old yellow, dingy one that comes up online, the one where she pushed her own friend, a friend to Gia since elementary school, headfirst into the toilet, dunking her down into the tank, forcing her entire body inside. Russ shivers with disgust thinking about the girl stuck in there, probably barfing and gagging and crying. And how horrible to then die slowly in a hospital with an infection. Although Russ wasn't in Seattle when this happened, plenty of people still talk to him about it. They ask him if Will still talks to Gia. He tells them no, no way.

Slumped, his hands on his hips, Will seems to struggle to find the words.

Russ remains still.

"She's sick," he finally says. "Like really sick. Weeks-to-live sick." He pinches the bridge of his nose. "She passes out, going into these mini comas."

Russ lets this soak in. The detail, the emotion—Will must have talked to her, maybe even seen her.

"I thought you and her weren't talking—"

"It's an autoimmune thing. It attacks the brain stem and her cells and her organs. It's brutal."

"You've talked to her?"

Will sighs. "I've never stopped talking to her." He grabs a rock from the sand, a gnarled, chunky stone, and skips it across the water. He could skip any rock, regardless of its shape or size. "We decided it would be best to pretend. I would make it seem like I hated her. Like I'd never speak to her again."

Rubbing both temples, Russ finds himself pacing.

"Logan doesn't believe that I cut it off," Will says. "I can tell."

Gia had been Will's girlfriend since the start of his freshman year—her sophomore year. That means the "fake" breakup happened sometime the next summer, after the push.

"We had to keep it to ourselves," Will says, snatching another rock from the sand. "Logan is fucking psycho." He hurls the rock so high it becomes a speck, then falls and dinks into the waters of the Sound.

Russ stops pacing. "I thought y'all were friends."

"There you go with the y'all. Your Texas takeaway." Will sighs. "Me and Logan pretend to be friends. But he can't stand me. And he downright hates Gia, of course."

It was odd why Logan remained friends with Will, or at least pretended to, but it's obvious why he hates her: the girl she pushed was the only person who ever really mattered to him, his girlfriend, Keely Cristy.

"He's always doing shit, you know," Will says, "trying to intimidate me, or embarrass me. Doing weird stuff too." Will looks to the sky, his eyes closed, giving his face to the raging sun until it looks like it might start to burn. "I mean what happened happened. I can't change it. But you know what's fucked up? Nobody ever gives a shit that Gia just lives every day in anguish and regret and would do anything to change it. And that she never meant to . . ."

"What kind of weird stuff?"

Will shakes his head. "I can't prove it."

"Like what?"

"Most of the stuff, it could be a coincidence, but there's one thing that happened a few days ago, after the news dropped about Gia's medical release. I found a dead bird—a crow—on the hood of my truck. It looked staged there, its neck all twisted backward."

Russ shudders, imagining the mangled creature.

"I don't think he'd actually do anything, but me and Gia won't be around to find out."

"Where are you going?"

"We've got to get her help. It's serious." He swigs and swallows. "Her dad—she barely knows him really, but

he's had the exact same condition for years, and somehow, he's survived. We've got to find him." He takes one
more drink. "After that, who knows. It just won't be here."

4

Logan kneels in the soil, the knees of his blue jeans dampening, his bare feet digging into the dirt. Shirtless, hands folded, he prays. He prays for forgiveness—not for what he's done, but for sins that are imminent.

This farm is his father's creation. Two acres' worth of peas, beans, and broccoli—all organic (or at least marketed that way to local grocery stores)—next to an acre pasture for free-range chickens, fenced in, with a formidable coop that Logan and his father built a decade ago, when Logan was a spry nine-year-old who could swing a hammer with surprising pop. The farm produced enough sustenance for meals and a meek income, sufficient for necessities: fuel, clothes, school supplies, and booze for Dad. The alcohol took its toll, however. Six months ago, just days after Logan's eighteenth birthday, his father's liver was finally scarred to death. Logan was left with a farm, no family, and no help.

A yellow ladybug explores the back of Logan's ankle, crawling over coarse black hair, as if the hair were blades of grass meshed in a meadow. As Logan lies forward onto his stomach, the bug flies off. The front of Logan's hardened torso, a long, muscular grid, settles into the damp dirt, freshly irrigated, the water having little time to soak, evaporating fast into the roasted air. Logan knows better than to water in the late afternoon, but it's his last chance.

His hands are his pillow. The coolness on his chest and the sun on his back are pure joy.

His father named this place S.R. Farm for two reasons: first, as an ode to the SR-71 reconnaissance plane Logan's grandad had flown in Vietnam, and second, for the Snoqualmie River, its flow within earshot, flowing south to the Puget Sound.

Although the farm was an hour from North Seattle High—two hours of lost work for Logan per round trip—his father signed the school zone variance form, conditioned on Logan continuing to fulfill his farm duties. For Logan, waking two hours earlier to complete his work was well worth the school change. Not that he particularly liked NSH—in fact, he hated the city—but he loved Keely Cristy, a girl from Seattle who'd attended a church retreat along the Snoqualmie, a two-week event where Logan served as a volunteer, and where they fell for each other.

Before he got a driver's license, Logan carpooled—mostly with farm customers and neighbors commuting to the city. Depending on who drove, and where they worked, they'd drop Logan at city bus stops for the final leg(s) of his daily trip to school. He got plenty of looks on the bus, his cowboy hat and boots out of place, like cattle strolling downtown. Once he joined the football team, he felt justified leaving the country-western clothes at home, choosing athletic gear instead. That lasted a couple of weeks, until Keely said she missed his real look.

Logan brought Keely to the farm as much as possible, away from the gossip and drama of high school to the safety and comfort of the crop field, surrounded by Sitka spruce, cedar trees, and ponderosa pines, where they would wrestle and play until tiring, lying out in the soil, the sunlight magic on her cheek, her smile the closest thing to heaven.

The yellow ladybug crawls by Logan's face, crawling over the dirt, over pebbles that to the bug are boulders. Logan sticks his finger in her way, and the bug's antennae tap the ridges in his skin as she climbs up and over, back into the soil, and flies off again, disappearing.

Keely's presence is strongest here: among the baby plants, as she called them, the fresh scent of wet dirt, the wobbly drips of water balancing on bushy leaves. Her presence, in the spiritual sense, is not an acceptable consolation. Her life, her goodness, was robbed by Gia, who—unbelievably—will be free in a matter of hours, free to reunite with Will.

Logan sniffs at the thought of him. Playing nice with Will, waiting for the right time, has been torture. Oh, what people must think: Logan Price is friends with Will Bayman? The same Will Bayman whose jealous girlfriend attacked Keely? Will Bayman, who according to the rumors, cheated with—

He springs to his feet, killing the thought, and storms toward the chicken's pasture, like a child stomping to his room, and at the same time like his inebriated father roaring down the hallway, belt in hand. Logan kicks the dirt, stubbing his toes and spraying bits of soil over leafy crops. He hobbles along, past the broccoli and the peas, the pain finally dissipating as he exits the field.

A fifty-pound sack of chicken feed leans against the pasture's gate post, the top half of the sack slumped over like a passed-out drunkard. With his right hand, Logan heaves the sack onto his shoulder, and with his left hand, he opens the gate. The chickens scurry toward him, clucking and bobbing their heads.

"Back up, you heathens," Logan says, ripping the top open, grabbing a handful of the grain-seed mixture and tossing it over the pasture. The chickens flock to the spread. Logan repeats this, hurling feed into the air, all around, like a king generously throwing bread to his hungry subjects, stopping only when the chickens are content, pecking away, unaware that more feed is even being hurled.

The old hen, Penny, pecks cautiously, taking feed and scanning her surroundings. She's been with Logan since the fourth grade, listening to him complain about kids at school, the no-good chickens of the flock, and his father. He picks her up, her head twisting side to side.

"You stay safe, Penny girl," Logan says, kissing her on the hackles, the feathers on her neck, and letting her down.

Stepping out with the sack slung over his shoulder, he clanks the gate shut. He drops the sack next to the post and leans over the steel frame, watching the birds pecking away, the chickens oblivious. From his back pocket, he takes papers—folded longways—and taps them against his palm. He opens the sack and sets them inside. Finally, he drops in a set of keys.

When Charles, the farm's only employee, opens the sack on Monday, he'll find his name on the farm deed. Hopefully the old man doesn't have a heart attack. Charles deserves the farm. And people should get what they deserve. Besides, he's the only one Logan knows who can tend to the crops and chickens.

Most people see Charles as a useless homeless man, but not Logan. Charles is a hell of a worker. And, more importantly, he's a good friend. After Logan's father died, Logan used the savings no longer wasted on alcohol to hire Charles. Ironically, the man now spends most of his pay on Miller Lite.

Logan walks to the house, a two-bedroom wood box, the only home he has known. In middle school, Logan had friends over twice. Both times, the kids—different kids—teased him about his mini house, his shack as they called it, and asked things like, "Do you shiver when using the outhouse?" The Prices had indoor plumbing, of course. But what those turds didn't know was that Logan could already fix plumbing. He knew carpentry, electrical, and welding, and he could run the farm equipment—the tractor and the mini excavator.

On the porch, there's a log with its center carved out, an unfinished canoe. Logan's father decided they would build it together, for fun. But Logan had already seen too many unfinished, do-it-together projects, like the new tool shed—where now only a concrete pad rests—or the new back porch, where vegetation has regrown over the area they cleared. Today, the log is nothing but an outdoor bed. Logan finds himself sleeping in it routinely, avoiding the quiet interior of the house, preferring the sounds of the critters, the leaves, the breeze.

Although he prefers sleeping outside, Logan hates the wicked oak tree across the gravel drive. Each morning, the sun illuminates the tree's sawed-off limb, reminding him, in his first thoughts of the day, of his failed attempt to kill himself. He remembers all the details, not just the noose around his neck—opening the A-frame ladder underneath the tree's canopy, slinging the rope over the limb, positioning himself, the hesitation before wobbling the ladder, preparing to kick it away, remorseful thoughts of Charles finding him, rageful thoughts of Will and Gia happy. Then changing his mind, trying to steady it, the ladder out of control. At the instant the ladder gave way, Logan slipped the noose off his head, falling with the ladder fifteen feet and smashing into the earth. He stood, unbroken but furious, as if the tree had pushed him. Logan reset the ladder. But instead of a rope, he carried up a chainsaw. He amputated its limb, as if the tree deserved it.

Eyeing the tree now, Logan bursts out of the canoe. He flings open the screen door, banging it against the dingy siding. He barges into the empty house, a twinge of mildew pervading the living room, but he can't smell it anymore; his nose is immune to the stench. Lit dimly through closed shutters, the guts of the home are basically unused, the living room seemingly abandoned, the process of ruin beginning.

The gym bag is already packed: tools, clothes, limited food, water, pistol, and most importantly, the remote, a detonator of sorts. He made the preparations last night, not only at the farm, but also at the kill site.

He zips closed the gym bag and dresses for the party: plain black swim trunks and a military-green tee, the shirt clinging to his jagged shoulders and rocky chest, outlining the gold cross hanging from his neck, the chain a gift from Keely for his fifteenth birthday. Logan fixes his hair with a plastic comb that's missing teeth in the middle. He tops his head with his cowboy hat and looks himself over in the full-length mirror.

Finished, Logan slings the gym bag over his shoulder and takes his phone and truck keys off the nightstand, where he set them next to a five-by-eight picture of Keely. He took the picture at the crest of Mt. Hood, and in it her hair trickles out from her beanie, her proud, loving smile on display. He stops and stares at the photo, then picks it up and brings it with him.

At the front door, Logan looks back on the small house. Nothing in it has ever changed. Always the same musty carpet, the same secondhand furniture, the lack of decorations. And though he's always hated the emptiness and the shame that came with this shack, it was the place he grew up.

With his gym bag and the picture, he leaves, for good.

5

Will and Russ are parked two blocks down from Rando's, and the street is stuffed with cars, thickest near the party. Russ takes in the neighborhood, the sun setting in pinks and blues. The oversized homes here are framed with wrought-iron fences, painted a blue-rust color, making them appear antique-like. But the homes, and their fences, were just built in the last ten years.

Russ bounces his leg, reminding himself again that he only needs to get through a few hours at the party. When it's time, he'll head out with Will. He can't imagine, however, that when Will drops him off, they'll really give each other a final goodbye. He glances at his friend, who is tapping on his phone. There's no way Will just up and leaves for good. No way Will just abandons his home forever, like some scared lion abandoning his territory and his pride. No way.

Russ texts his mom for the second time since leaving the Coop. Still no reply. The ride out of the Coop was silent, awkward, Russ taking it in: Gia and her condition,

Logan and the dead crow, Will's worry and his plan to desert Seattle.

By the time they swung by Russ's apartment and then got to Will's house, the awkwardness had faded, but it remained in the background like a dull white noise. Inside Will's, they prepped for the party. Will, despite the Jägermeister buzz, completed four sets of dumbbell presses, flys, and curls, while Russ scrolled on his phone, familiarizing himself—although it was difficult—with the comments on the video, the spank jokes, the ridicule, getting ahead of what was to come at the party.

Will kills the truck's engine. Bass, drifting from Rando's, vibrates the cab. Russ glances at his friend, who flips down his visor, using the mirror to inspect his teeth and nostrils for unwanted guests.

Russ examines his last text, to his mom: *Going to Rando's with Will. See you later. Travel safe.*

Travel safe? What teenager says travel safe? Wait, he thinks, teenager? Technically, yes, eighteen is a teenager, but really, he's an adult now. At first, instead of travel safe, he had typed, *Love you*, but he deleted it. Those words are too risky. His mom rarely says them, pretty much never, and after the embarrassment she suffered from his graduation, reciprocation is unlikely, even implausible. Maybe she was right. Hell, maybe Eckspun was too. Russ should have acted like a valedictorian.

Russ waits for the three dots to appear, the ones that indicate someone is typing back. But the dots don't come. On the screen, his cursor blinks. It's the only thing moving. It's steady, like the tick-tock of a clock. It's not unusual for his mother not to reply. In fact, Russ could scroll through the text thread and probably find seven of his messages to every one of hers.

As a child, when his mom would get angry, Russ played a guessing game: guessing—or estimating—how long she might stay mad. He kept a notebook, tracking her anger spells in frequency and length, comparing results against correlated predetermined factors such as the seriousness of the offense (a.k.a., what Russ did to piss her off), her overall mood prior to the offense, weekly alcohol consumption, boyfriend status, and the frequency of their lover-spats. Using the collected data, Russ modified certain factors and the overall equation, tinkering with the formula over and over, until he dialed in the error rate to within three hours. Impressively, he could make successful estimations despite the unusually long spans she tended to remain angry. It was normal for her anger episodes to last multiple weeks.

Clicking off his phone, tired of the screen, the waiting, and the social media comments—and having once before accidentally jumped into Rando's pool with a phone in his pocket—Russ tosses the device, wrapped in an orange case, into the glove box and closes the stitched leather door.

He and Will both step out of the truck, properly dressed for the pool party: Russ sporting board shorts, tapered to the knee, Will rocking pink Chubbies, the hem tight against his quad. Sprinklers spray, watering lush lawns, stretching from the iron fencing to the circular driveways made of pewter-colored pavers. They stroll up the sidewalk, stepping over sprinkler puddles, through the scent of water on hot concrete. Will holds his head high, his eyes on the party house, scanning for classmates. Russ, on the other hand, is looking down, a half step off his friend's pace, staring at his new Nikes—Supreme X Airforce Ones with red laces—a graduation gift, perhaps a farewell gift, from Will. The sidewalk grooves remind Russ of J-Jack and the *kerchunk* of his wheeled trash cans. Of course, that leads to thoughts about Russ's speech and the reality that an onslaught of mockery lies ahead.

What did J-Jack think of his speech? Odds are the video has already come his way, the new retiree probably watching it while chilling in his backyard—his sanctuary, as he described it—in the quiet with a stirred drink. Russ imagines him setting the phone down, shaking his head, closing his eyes, letting the sounds of the birds fall around him, letting the falling sun fade away. Russ wishes he was the retired janitor, not the new graduate with his life's story forever marred.

As Russ and Will approach Rando's, the boom of the music intensifies, and hoots and hollers shoot through the beat like invisible fireworks.

Randy "Rando" FitzRoy is best known for his parties. His reputation is owed to his parents, who turn a blind eye to these events, pretending to know nothing of the gatherings—for liability reasons. They open their estate to wild young adults, doing things they—Mr. and Ms. FitzRoy—never had the pleasure of doing, having been brought up in snobby, overly strict households. Their upbringings were also the reason they decided Randy—never calling him Rando, a nickname they didn't hate but didn't love—would attend public school. Although the FitzRoy residence is not a mansion, it's impressive nonetheless with its seven bedrooms, home gym, home theater, and bowling alley, in addition to the pool.

As Will and Russ enter through the FitzRoys' wrought-iron gate, they follow the famous torches along the pathway. Before each party, the torches—solar LED landscaping lights made to look like flames—are skewered into the lawn, demarcating the way to the backyard. The torches flicker like Russ's nervous system, the intensity oscillating, his body flashing hot between breaths, a vomit-feeling rising. As they get closer, the beat gets louder, the bass like a war drum, vibrating his guts. He swallows hard and follows Will into the back yard like a shadow, wishing he could be just that.

As if walking out onto a stage, Will presents himself, arms spread. Instantly, someone points and shouts, "Willie-B!"

Will stops, and Russ almost smacks into him. People are everywhere, and they all turn. Under the paper lanterns strewn above them, they chant, for the second time that day: "Wil-lee B! Wil-lee B! Wil-lee B!"

Will raises his arms high, as if taking in one last mass showing of love from his biggest fans. Then, he sidesteps and turns to Russ, and like a showman, he bends backward, revealing his best friend. Without saying a word, Will tells his people: here is your hero. The people's chant morphs as they point at Russ, awe on their faces. The new chant, messy at first, becomes clear in seconds: "Red-Butt Russ! Red-Butt Russ! Red-Butt Russ!"

Russ is like a bug whose shelter, whose rock, has been ripped away, leaving him exposed and small. The nerve fibers in his feet want him to scurry, but Russ stands there taking the public shaming, taking what he deserves. As his mother would say, he's made his own bed. His face blushes, and he can feel the heat in his cheeks and the sweat percolating on his forehead. Here stands Red-Butt-Russ and his red face.

Russ wants to lower his head, to hide his burning mug, but he doesn't. To his credit, he faces the crowd, on full display. In doing so, however, in meeting eye to eye all the individual faces of the mob, he realizes this is not a shaming. This, contrarily, is congratulatory in nature, a cheer, a showing of respect. This mob, his friends, are not laughing at him as they pump their fists. No, instead, they make eye contact with him, nod at him, displaying intense game-faces as if he just scored a touchdown.

That said, he now has a new, not-so-desirable nickname. But he can live with it. Fuck it. From this day forth, may he be known as Red-Butt Russ. With full acceptance, a smile grows on his face, but it's short lived, dropping away as cell phones aim at him. The thought of another video for the internet makes his insides squirm, until he realizes this is an opportunity. Red-Butt Russ is no victim. He's a victor, having outsmarted and slayed the fire-breathing dickhead they call Explosion. And so, Russ pumps his fist back at the crowd, sending the volume higher. The crowd explodes—surely sending the video(s) shaking. Hysterically, the crowd swarms Red-Butt Russ, a mass of warm bodies, alcohol breath, spittle flying on everyone. It's like a group hug, but with people jumping, hollering, spilling, while the crowd showers Russ with praise, as if he took one for the team, sacrificing himself to beat the man.

When the swarm breaks, Russ finds himself under the cabana, practically carried there, a beer placed in his hand. Hip-hop beats resurface and the partygoers get back at it, ready for the next spectacle.

Coming toward Russ is the host, open-palmed and grinning. On Rando's forearm is a tattoo of black sun-glasses, with *fun times* spelled out in the lenses. Even at night, Rando always wears shades. If not on his eyes, or the tip of his nose, he wears them on his forehead or clipped on his shirt. "Sup you crazy mothafuckin' vale-dictorian son-of-a-bitch," Rando says, clasping Russ's hand.

Next to Rando is Sandra Berks in a cardinal-red bikini, cardinal red being the school color of Stanford, where she'll start in the fall. She hugs Russ, her shoulders smelling of vanilla sunscreen, baked in and warm.

As Sandra pats Russ's back, Rando stands behind her, peering over his shades, looking her up and down, pop-ping his eyebrows twice. "Josh coming?" Rando asks.

She lets go of Russ. "He was," she says, shrugging. "We'll see." Sandra pats Russ's shoulder. "Well, I guess even if I had won the V spot, I couldn't have beat that speech."

For the last year, Russ and Sandra have been competi-tors. She didn't know it at first, as Russ was a stealthy academic achiever. He never told people his grades or participated in the well-known extracurricular activities that most ambitious students took, like student government and debate. Although, he did sign up for the astronomy club. If anyone asked, however, he would say he had to join for the credits. The truth: Russ loved investigating the cosmos. He would spend nights on the roof of his apartment with his telescope, partly to get away from his mom and her boyfriend(s), but mostly to look out into the infinite. That's where he'd do most of his journaling, something recommended by J-Jack after Russ returned from Texas.

Before Russ can reply, Rando says, "Woah whoa whoa whoa, what do you mean win the V spot? And how do I play?"

"Valedictorian," Russ says. "V spot for short."

"Never mind. I don't want to play."

Russ grins. "I'm sure your speech would have been much more uplifting," he says to Sandra. He takes a drink but keeps his eyes on hers.

"Probably." She smiles. "But much more boring, and way less meaningful."

Russ chokes down his beer. "Meaningful? That's a nice way to say it."

"Hey, Russ," Rando says, butting in. "How you like the ambiances?" He swipes his finger over the backyard, over the transparent balloons with their tiny lights hanging down like jellyfish tentacles, over the giant white balls floating in the water, over the manicured shrubs, shaped precisely into what look like lollipops.

Subtly, so as not to poke fun at Rando's misuse of language but to let Sandra know he caught it, Russ says, "Uh, yeah, great ambiances."

Sandra smacks her lips closed to keep from laughing.

"The fucking pool light's out, though," Rando says, shaking his head. "Like we don't pay these pool dorks enough."

Russ looks it over and says, "The dark water gives it a freaky vibe, though—you know … it kind of contrasts nicely with all the ambiences."

Sandra laughs to a snort. At the same time, Rando says, "Ohhh . . . my man, Red-Butt Russ likes the freaky." He grabs Russ around his shoulders.

Splash after splash hits the pool, partiers gushing down the slide, going headfirst, stacked in twos, while others cannonball off the diving board.

"Yeah, boi!" Rando shouts, after Oumar—a foreign exchange student beloved by all—double flips. "I've gotta give my homie props." Rando fist-bumps Russ and skips to the pool.

Russ and Sandra take sips at the same time.

"So," she says, "you're opening an investment firm, huh, no college?"

"Why wait, you know? I'm just going for it."

She looks down at her red toenails. "I got to ask. If not for college, why go for valedictorian?"

The truth is, Russ didn't set out for it. The challenge came to him. J-Jack was the one who suggested it early in his freshman year. He even gave Russ the rules, printed with specific highlights.

Russ shrugs. "I can't say."

Sandra rolls her eyes playfully. She's much brighter than Russ, and he knows it. Sandra being salutatorian obviously bothers her, but she's being a good sport.

"Well," she says, clutching his bicep, "you deserve it."

Sandra holds his arm for an extra second, then abruptly removes it, as if she's been spotted doing something wrong. She smiles and walks to the pool.

With a confused look, Russ turns around.

Tara.

6

No matter the occasion, Tara integrates her rich-girl rocker style, preppy and rebellious. Tonight, she's jeweled more than usual: five rings, a mix of bright, dainty gemstones and two gothic pieces—a curved silver feather and a graphite band topped with a gold five-pointed star. On her midriff, a white body chain snakes around her abs between white bikini bottoms and a matching crop top with one shoulder strap, a tattoo running underneath it, a long line of tiny, angry fireflies spreading from the nape of her neck to her wrist.

"Russell Burton," she says from the sliding glass door at the rear of the cabana, her tone like a mother scolding a child. "Who do you think you are?"

Russ arches an eyebrow as Tara saunters to him. Eyeing him face-to-face, she slides her fingers up the back of his hair. Standing high on her tiptoes, with their glittery blue toenails, she lengthens her body, her neck, and presses her glossed lips onto his cheek. The wet spot left behind makes Russ tingle.

Tara wags her finger against his chest. "You think you can pull a stunt like that without telling me first?"

Russ isn't sure if she's serious. "You didn't like my speech?"

"Not the part about me."

Behind Russ, in the pool, partiers flip air mattresses, flinging new-adult girls into the water. On the flagstone pool deck, new-adult boys whack each other with pool noodles.

"But you were in the stands nodding at me."

"Uh, yeah, you were frozen up there. I was encouraging you to go on, not to bring me into it."

"Wait, wait, Eckspun got what he deserved, right?"

Tara smirks, shaking her head. "If we're being honest, did I not deserve expulsion?"

"What? No, of course not. Expulsion for what, art? Like you said, he ruined you."

"Ruined me?"

"That's what you said, remember?"

"Come on Russ, that's dramatic." She folds her arms, pushing up her cleavage, perhaps intentionally, perhaps not.

Russ tries not to look, aiming his gaze high on her smoky eyelids and long lashes, spread like geisha fans.

"I painted the freaking administration building," she says, "without permission."

"Are you serious right now?"

"I'm just being real. Besides, the midnight mural—that's what some people are calling it—made Dr. Eckspun look like a creep. What was he supposed to do?"

"He is a creep."

Russ shouldn't be surprised at this flip-flop, at Tara first saying she was ruined then saying she deserved expulsion. Since freshman year, since he first met her, Tara has done nothing but oscillate: from being a cheerleader to a skater, from having boyfriends then girlfriends and back to boyfriends, from extreme sports to fashion design and art—though never giving up jet-ski racing—from being a good friend to being too cool for everyone, from being a rebel to being noble and real.

"To take away your graduation," Russ says. "I mean, how many murals had you already painted?"

"You know how many." Tara takes a sharp sip off her straw and checks the crowd behind Russ.

He unblocks her view and faces the same way. "I guess it is what it is."

"Yep. You'll be Red-Butt Russ for the rest of your life."

Russ swigs. He slides his knuckles across his wet lips. "Well, at least I tried."

"Yeah? And what exactly were you trying to do?"

"Actually? I was trying to give Eckspun what he—"

"You weren't trying to impress?"

"What?"

"Be honest. Keep it real, okay."

In front of them, Will is on the far side of the pool deck, commanding an audience, mimicking himself holding the microphone, reenacting the Molbeck fall, ten or so partiers laughing their asses off. Tara smiles.

"So," Russ says, clearing his throat, "before I got Eckspun to . . . react . . . were you with it?"

She scoffs. "With it? I'm not sure what that means. Impressed? No. Except that you made valedictorian. Now that's something, and really the only reason I even went. My mom loved it though, I got to say. She only went to stare down Eckspun, to eff with him, but she got something much better, and she couldn't care less if it was at your expense."

This was worse than he imagined. Tara is not only unimpressed and unsupportive, but seemingly irritated, no, embarrassed by the speech. Russ's effort, his try, didn't matter. The spectacle, the spanking, was detrimental. Did he deserve this? To make it worse, just look at Will. How did he figure it all out? It's like he's immune to embarrassing himself. Just look at him. Look at all these people feeding off his energy—his grand presence—all of them oblivious, not knowing he'll be leaving for good, that this is their last time to have at him. They'll all miss him, but no one as much as Russ.

"Anyways," Tara says. "So, you want to be one of those stockbroker guys?"

Russ doesn't answer.

"Oh, come on," she says, "don't be like that." She whacks his chest playfully.

"Like what?"

Rolling her eyes, she says, "Uh, all mad and shit."

"Why would I be mad? You're just keeping it real."

"Exactly." Tara looks from side to side, as if she's searching for an escape route.

Russ hopes she finds one.

Will finishes his reenactment, pretending to jump off the graduation stage, as he did when Mr. Ziegler, Ms. Molbeck's defender, ran him off. While his audience laughs, Will glances at Russ and Tara. He fist bumps someone and moves toward the cabana, to Russ's relief.

"What's up with you two?" Will asks.

Before either can respond, a raspy voice behind them says, "Yeah, what the hell's up?"

Delighted, Tara spins into Logan Price, wrapping her arms around his ribs and burying her face in his chest.

"Somebody needed a hug," Logan says, rubbing her back. "You alright?"

She stays on him for a moment more. "I'm good. I'm just going to miss you, Logy."

Logan places his arm around Tara's shoulders. "Well, this being our last NSH party, we need one last chicken fight, right?"

"Oh, no way, I'm not getting in the pool," Tara says. "This suit is for looks only."

"That's what you always say." Logan shakes her gently. "Come on." He up-nods at Will. "Will, you're down, right?"

Will mulls it over. "Yeah," he says, tossing his arm over the back of Russ's neck. "I'll take this guy."

Russ furrows his brow. "Me on you?" He knows what Will is trying to do—trying to get Russ physical contact with Tara, something playful. He probably feels bad for telling him to forget her. But playfighting with Tara is the last thing Russ wants right now.

"If you're more of a bottom guy," Will says, "I'll take the top."

"I'm definitely not a bottom guy."

Will pats Russ's shoulder twice. "It's on!"

"Not with me, it's not," Tara says. "I was really just stopping by. I've got to get up early."

Logan looks at her sideways. "It hasn't been one day past graduation and you're already turning into your parents?"

"I'm meeting my dad for breakfast, before I fly out."

"Maybe Sandra wants in," Russ says.

"Pfff, please," Tara says, "she'd fall off Logan like a piece of fuzz."

"Okay then." Logan raises his eyebrows. "You're my topper."

Tara doesn't disagree.

Logan continues, "Traditional rules: the loser's pledge skinny-jumps into the pool."

"I'll be our pledge," Will says, volunteering to take the skinny-jump should they lose, saving Russ the possibility of additional embarrassment today.

"Tara pledges for us," Logan says.

"Pfff, you know you're our pledge," Tara says. "But it doesn't really matter because I won't lose."

Logan takes off to the pool. "Chicken Fiiiiiight!"

Like a pack of wild dogs wagging their tails around a feed site, the partiers crowd the edges of the water, adding to the smell of chlorine and air-filled rubber toys the stench of beer burps and sweat and fading sunscreen.

Russ puts his shoes onto a lawn chair under the cabana. Emptying his pockets, he places his wallet and AirPods inside the Nikes. Then he folds his shirt and places it atop his shoes. He heads for the pool, trying not to shake.

Logan sits on the pool's bottom step, submerging himself to his armpits. Tara follows him in but stays standing. Onlookers remove inflatable pool-toys, clearing the dark water of obstructions. The last to be removed is a long, red, blown-up hot dog.

Logan reaches for Tara, grabbing the back of her thighs, his wet hands pressing into her dry skin. He lifts her up, over his head, setting her carefully onto his shoulders.

To load Russ, Will backs up to the pool's wall, like a truck docking. On the pool deck, Russ, instead of loading directly onto Will's shoulders, sits behind him and has to drag his backside forward, reminding himself of his cocker spaniel that would drag its hindquarters all over the apartment, earning a one-way-ticket to the pound.

Logan rises, Tara's legs wrapped under his shoulders, her feet on the small of his back, one ankle clutching the other, locked in. Logan marches to the pool's center.

Around the pool deck, five or six phones record. Recording chicken fights is allowed, but recording a skinny-jump would get you banished from the party house.

Dangling his legs over Will's shoulders, Russ struggles to keep balanced, unsure if—and where—he should hold, resisting the urge to grab Will's head. Russ is a virgin chicken fighter, having avoided all of them, other than as a spectator, during his time at NSH.

Will grips Russ's dangling ankles, steadying him. With a spirited grin, Will hauls Russ toward the center, toward their opponents and their serious faces, faces on the verge of growling. As Will steps into the deeper water, the pool's bottom steepening, Russ's backside slips down. He panics, flailing, grabbing for his friend and smacking Will's forehead with wet palms.

"Woah, I can't see, bro," Will says as Russ's pinkies press on his eyelids. "Relax, relax. I got you."

The crowd laughs as Russ repositions himself onto Will's shoulders.

Logan begins to circle the oncoming enemy. Tara puts her fists up, guarding her face like a fighter, except that her palms are outward, like she's a cat ready to scratch. Logan accelerates his circling, the water whirlpooling.

Will moves against the grain of the current, instigating a collision. Logan attacks, ramming Will's chest, jostling the big man, who is not accustomed to being jostled. Will's nostrils flare, and he bangs back into Logan, but Logan, driving his legs forward, equalizes the blow.

With both fists, Tara strikes Russ's shoulders, knocking him off balance, his butt sliding off Will's shoulders again. But this time he stays there. As she strikes a second blow, Russ grabs her hands, and their fingers interlace. Resisting the urge to squeeze them, Russ shoves her arms away instead.

Presumably, this will be the last chicken fight in a long line of chicken fights over the last four years at Rando's. And Tara is undefeated, her perfect record on the line. She entered more chicken fights than most, and she always won, sending pledge after pledge to the plank. Usually it was girls, the ones with liquid courage, challenging her, but she's beaten two boys too, one supposedly going easy on her—whatever—and the other one, who was richly overconfident, taken by surprise when Tara, from his rear, installed a choke hold, her rock-climbing-built bicep flexing into his windpipe, forcing a tap out.

Thirsty for violence, the crowd roots for Tara. Moreover, particularly for the girls, Will makes for a fine skinny-jump pledge. The crowd cheers: "Get him," "Dump him," "Yeah!" Tara strikes, landing a right-hand jab to Russ's sternum. His breath pops like a balloon. He gasps, pain erupting from his lungs. The crowd explodes.

Perhaps without realizing Russ is straining above, Will charges at Logan, the water whooshing around the big man's chest. Russ manages to gulp air as he leans forward, widening his arms, preparing to wrestle.

Moments before contact, Logan side-steps, dodging the attack. Like a boxer, he bounces backward into shallower water, keeping Will to his front, in the deep end, forcing his enemy to stand on the steepest slope of the pool's bottom. Logan knows this pool well—not just the slope, but also the workings of the filters, pumps, and lighting—having done handyman work for the FitzRoys.

Resembling a bull missing the matador's red cape, Will slows, angles back toward Logan, and attacks full force uphill. Logan waits, his hands below the surface. As Will closes the distance, Logan slings his arms forward, firing two waves at Will's face. Then, stiffening his arms ahead like two battering rams, Logan slams his fists into Will's chest, the impact forcing Will backward into deeper water, forcing his rider to lose his balance, his grip, sending Russ flying off backward, splashing into the pool.

Sinking, his lungs on fire, Russ is disoriented. Underwater, the crowd's roar is muffled, but it serves as a guide to the surface. As Russ emerges, coughing out the metallic taste of chlorinated water, Tara raises her arms over him in victory, pumping her fists, tapping her heels on Logan's stomach.

In a low voice, Will asks, "You alright?"

Russ nods, a look of squeamishness on his face, as if he's about to barf up pool water. But with all the phones recording, that's not an option.

"Okay, time to pay up," Will says, breast-stroking toward the shallow end.

Russ follows.

As they climb the steps, water falls off them. On the pool deck, Will smiles for the cameras and immediately makes his way to the diving board. Russ positions himself in the thick of the crowd, the only place to hide.

Tara celebrates as Logan floats her to the wall. She climbs off of him, only her legs wet. Logan climbs out to pats on the back.

Will stands on the diving board, thumbs in his waist band. "Phones off," he says, checking that every device is lowered and stowed. Satisfied, Will whips down his shorts, stepping over them, standing bare. Not all the girls react the same: some sip drinks to cover their heartbeats, some pretend not to look, some stare open-mouthed, and the most honest just bite their bottom lip. Will thumps his chest like a gorilla. The crowd hoots and hollers, raising glasses.

Will sprints, barreling along the diving board, his feet stomping, his strides increasing, lunging, jumping up, his toes landing perfectly at the edge, loading and flexing the board. As it recoils, Will's massive body springs into the air, leaving the board wobbling, almost warping. At his highpoint, he gracefully forms a pike position, seeming to hang in midair for more than a moment over the dark water.

As Will's pike unfolds, his body straightening, diving down, the water illuminates, translucent blue, but flickering.

As if the pool lighting is part of the show, the crowd oohs and aahs.

He cuts through the water, a perfect dive. The crowd roars, their excitement building as Will stays under: ten seconds, twenty seconds, thirty. Then everyone begins to quiet.

The water turns dark, and the crowd's excitement changes to concern: "Oh my God," "Is he ok?" "Somebody do something." Logan jumps into the pool, swimming across the surface then thrusting under the water. Russ circles the edge, weaving between spectators, his legs shaking. Will has been under for nearly a minute. Should he jump in too?

Logan appears at the surface, straining. "Help me! he yells, trying to catch his breath. "Get him out!"

Bodies jump in, Russ first, splashing around Will's stiff frame, the horde frantic, raising the boy's body onto the pool deck.

<h1 style="text-align:center">7</h1>

Eyes hover over Will like flying saucers. His face is expressionless, frozen, as if he's hypnotized. He seems to behold the darkness above him as if looking past everyone, as if finding something profound between the stars in the deep black emptiness. The burnt-hair-smell is disturbing, as is Will's lack of eye contact. Will is someone who peers into you, someone who is always present, noticing everyone, never lost in his mind. But now, he's vegetative.

Kneeling on the flagstone, Logan thrusts his palm into Will's chest, repeating mechanically, "Come on. You better fight, Bayman."

Hoverers join in: "Come on, Will. Fight. Come on bro."

Russ hangs over Will's bloated body, his hands squeezing the back of his own head, his eyes bulging red. Telepathically, Russ begs Will to wake. *You have to get up, you have to.* But it's like Russ is asking a dead person to come alive. And although Russ has never seen a dead body, Will looks as lifeless as anything he can imagine. His skin is gray, his consciousness gone.

With each thrust into Will's chest, there's a squeak, like a moan. Logan stays steady, pumping, pumping, pumping.

Outside the hovering eyes, around the pool deck and under the cabana, frantic graduates shout into their phones, pleading for help to 911, demanding the ambulance hurry. Others cry into their phones to their parents, trying to explain what happened but not fully making sense, their voices cracking, yelping, like they're children lost in grocery stores.

Finally, in the distance, sirens wail, arriving over horns blaring, emergency lights flashing on dark homes, flashing with the same intensity as the fear pulsing inside Russ. Two paramedics rush from an ambulance to the backyard, holding orange bags, their long hair pulled back tight. Surveying the scene, they jog to Will. The most senior paramedic leads, her neck wrinkled from stress and strain. She barks for people to move back and then demands answers, asking anyone she can find what happened. As she takes over CPR, deploying a resuscitation mask with a hand pump, she listens to reports of the flickering pool light. "Weak pulse," she says to arriving medics rolling in a stretcher, "possible electric shock."

Police push back the crowd, extending the perimeter around Will. As Russ walks backward, the feeling in his legs disappears, but he keeps moving, as if he's just floating away, a drifting balloon, uncontrolled. Will getting farther from him, smaller.

Officers herd the stunned graduates into groups in different areas, directing them—you and you this way, you in the red shirt, over here. Some graduates are directed under the cabana, some into the pool house, some onto the front lawn. The police shout, not because the teen-adults are defiant, but because they're confused, their minds in shock, not easily able to follow directions.

The back of Russ's knee collides with a lawn chair. He falls, his backside bouncing onto the taut fabric.

The paramedics raise the stretcher, lifting Will, jostling his enormous body. They rush him away, leaving behind a wet spot and remnants of emergency equipment, scraps of packaging, and a small, soiled cloth pad.

Russ sits motionless until an officer directs him off the chair. Next to Russ, one chair over, are his shirt and shoes. He gathers his belongings and uses the shirt to cover his face. As Russ sobs into it, he follows the sound of the crowd into the pool house.

Russ squeezes inside. An officer comes in behind him, sliding the glass door shut.

"Listen up," the officer says, a vein popping out the side of his bald head as he marches through the crowd to the front, to the bar, a stack of papers in his hand. "There are highly trained medical staff tending to your friend, okay? So right now, we are going to do what we have to do to get you out of here. You are going to be given a statement form and a pen. I need everyone to write down what happened tonight. Make sure you fill out the contact section completely—your address, your cell phone. Once you're done, you'll give the form to me before leaving. And if anyone drives a vehicle out of here under the influence, they'll be arrested."

As Russ waits for his form, he slips his shirt on, the fabric comforting like a hug, except for the wet spots—wet from tears—which stick to his chest. The pool house is bright, the dimmers at maximum intensity, and his eyes have to adjust. Outside, a separate group of graduates sit under the cabana, filling out forms, some using the backs of their friends, others using the flagstone.

As Russ wiggles his foot into his shoe, someone passes him a pen and paper, a ticket out of here. Russ presses the form against the glass door and begins writing his name. Behind him, people sob, saying over and over, "I can't believe it, oh my God." One girl prays out loud.

Praying has always perplexed Russ, especially out loud, in public, the way people do when they're in trouble. Why not pray out loud when things are great? Because those people look crazy. And if they're crazy, so are the ones praying out loud because they're scared.

For the cabana group, an officer with a long chin leads them, giving directions and taking slips nonchalantly like a chaperone on a field trip.

Behind the long-chinned officer, near the pool, Logan speaks with the sergeant, a thin man with three pointed stripes on his sleeve. Logan leads him to the diving board and points to the water, to the pool light below the surface, recessed in the pool's wall. The sergeant shines his flashlight at it. As he squats down, angling the flashlight, the entire pool illuminates, flickering, like a strobe light. He jumps to his feet and tilts his head into the radio on his shoulder.

Inside the pool house, from the bald officer's radio, the sergeant's orders transmit:

"Dispatch, 8L90, we need power shut off to the pool."

"8L90, Seattle Fire is on scene and can assist. Stand-by."

Russ finishes writing his phone number. He pats his pockets, realizing his phone is in the truck, realizing his mom has no idea what's happened, and Will's mom might just now be finding out. A wave of urgency rips through him, and he begins scribbling down what he witnessed: the chicken fight, the skinny-jump, Logan diving in, Russ following, Logan giving CPR. What he doesn't write, but what crosses his mind, are the things Will said before the party: Gia getting out of prison, Logan acting weird, the dead crow on Will's truck. But how could Logan set up this accident? Impossible. And why would he then save Will?

"8L90, Dispatch, Seattle Fire is locating the circuit breaker."

"10-4"

"Also, do we have a contact for the homeowner?"

The bald officer makes an announcement: "I need anyone who lives at this residence to come forward."

The crowd turns to Rando, who's sitting in the corner, sunglasses on, talking quietly on his cell phone.

"You," the officer says, "What's your name?"

"Randy FitzRoy," he says, standing, the phone still glued to his ear.

"Make your way up. Who are you speaking to?"

Rando whispers into the phone, "He wants to know who I'm talking to."

"Is that your parents?"

"Yes."

"Let me have the phone."

"He wants the phone."

Rando walks up and hands it over. The officer taps the screen for the speaker, sets the phone on the bar, and readies his pen and notebook. "This is Officer Prenskey. Who am I speaking with?"

"Jenna FitzRoy." Her voice crackles through the phone. "I understand there was an accident, Officer. Is everyone okay?"

"Ma'am, are you aware there's a party going on here?"

"I am now. Me and my husband are two hours away. Is someone hurt?"

"Yes, someone was injured and transported to the hospital. We need you to come to the residence."

"Yes, of course—we'll be there as soon as possible."

Russ slips through the crowd, up to the officer, and offers his statement. The officer, still engaged with Mrs. FitzRoy, takes it and nods.

Russ heads for the front door, weaving through the graduates, their faces tense, distraught. As he makes his way through, saying, "Excuse me" at least three times, a soft hand grabs his.

"I'm going with you," Tara says, squeezing his fingers, holding on tight as if she might otherwise slip away. Without a word, Russ pulls her through the packed room, down a short hallway, to the black iron front door. They exit next to the garage, onto the oversized pewter-paved driveway, thick with confused graduates. Russ just stands there, not sure where to go. He has no ride. He came with Will.

And it's then he fully realizes the seriousness of the situation—that Will isn't here, that it was Will on that stretcher, Will Bayman the unbreakable, the unbeatable, Will clinging to life, his body like a zombie version of himself.

"I need to get to the hospital," Russ says, "but I don't have a ride."

Tara leans into his chest, her skin cold with goose-bumps. Russ wraps his arms around her, and they hold each other, trying to displace the helplessness inside.

"Come on," Tara says, releasing suddenly, as if a terrible thought crossed her mind. She grabs Russ's hand, leading him around the chaos of the driveway, to the torchlit sidewalk and out of the gate. She moves up the street like a power-walker, Russ hustling to keep pace, neighbors watching from their windows and porches. Tara looks back to check they're not being followed.

As they approach her Tesla, she lets go of Russ's hand and scampers to the driver's side.

Russ waits at the trunk. "You okay to drive to the hospital?"

"Come on, get in," she says.

As he slides inside and shuts the door, the chaos outside mutes. It's as if they're in a protective bubble.

"I'm fine," she says. "I didn't drink."

Russ saw her drink. "I thought you had . . . never mind."

She starts the car. "Just because it looks like a drink doesn't mean it is."

"Forget I said anything," Russ says, buckling his seatbelt. "I was thinking of what that cop said."

It's funny, though. Just earlier today, Russ and Will drank plenty. And afterward, Russ jumped in the truck, no questions asked, because Will was untouchable. Nothing bad ever happened to him.

Tara reaches into the back seat, grabbing shorts and a T-shirt. She unclips her body chain and chucks it into the back. Propped up in the console, her phone buzzes, the screen lighting up: *Logy*. She doesn't answer as she slips her clothes over her swimsuit. "We're not going to the hospital," she says.

Russ shifts in his seat. "What do you mean?"

"They won't let us see him right now anyway."

"We should be there."

Tara clicks in her seatbelt. "Do you think Will would want us to let Gia stand outside the prison, just waiting, wondering?"

Of course he wouldn't. No one else is coming for her. Both of her parents are estranged.

"Should you drop me off first? Gia doesn't even know me."

"She knows me. And there's no time." Tara tugs on the gear shifter, putting the car in drive. "We'll get her and go from there. That's what Will would want, right?"

Russ nods.

8

Razor wire corkscrews along the top of steel fencing, separating the parking lot from the prison yard, dividing the good from the bad. Inside the yard, floodlights illuminate the dead, patchy grass and the empty exercise equipment lying under a stubby guard tower. In the parking lot, streetlamps hum over a sheet of empty stalls and the five cars scattered there, everything lit in a dim orange.

The Tesla points at the release center, a faded red-brick building. Between the car and the entrance door are three rows of empty parking spaces and a sidewalk, a pitted concrete "red carpet" for the soon-to-be-parolees.

Russ's gut is tight, as if the heaviness of the prison is pressing on him. He wipes his palms across his shorts and lowers his window. A breeze strokes his face, cooling the sweat on his temples. He wiggles out a chill. Seven or eight parking spaces away, a woman in a miniskirt—white spandex coating her backside like fondant on a cake—shrieks and dances, her friend jumping and shrieking back.

A text message dings Tara's phone. She clicks the volume button down, silencing notifications, as she studies the screen. Russ pats his pockets, checking for his cell. It's still in Will's truck. His mom has probably texted by now, but she may not even know yet what's happened.

The wind rattles the metal fencing and blows a damp napkin into the air, pasting it against the chain links. Two concrete flowerpots squat at the outside edges of the entrance to the sidewalk leading to the glass entry door. In each, scraggly bushes cling to life in dehydrated soil. Sitting on a pot's edge, a man with dense gray hair, buzzed high and tight, picks fuzz off his collar with one hand, holding yellow tulips in his other, the petals glowing bright against the dull, decaying brick building.

Rubbing his eyes, Russ yawns. The prison comes back into view, and the tightness in his stomach spreads up to his chest and throat. He glances at Tara. She doesn't look up from her phone. Although Russ is eager to know what's going on, part of him doesn't want to. It could be bad news—that Will is now a vegetable or has the mind of a two-year-old.

Tara concentrates on the screen.

"Everything okay?" Russ finally asks.

"He's in Intensive Care," she says. "They're not letting anyone see him."

The gray, bloated body drifts through Russ's mind again. He shakes the thought. "Who are you texting with?"

Tara crosses and uncrosses her ankles. "A lot of people," she says, squirming into a new position, folding her legs under herself. "Hold on one second."

Russ shifts his focus to the entrance. In minutes, prisoners will be coming out. He cringes at the thought of Gia finding that Will isn't here, and worse, discovering his condition.

"Umm . . ." Tara says, keeping her attention on the screen. "There's too many people at the hospital. They're asking everyone to leave but family."

"Who all's there?"

"I'm not sure," she says, typing, "but we've got to figure out what to do with Gia."

Russ unbuckles. "Well, she's basically family, right? She's Will's—"

"It's not going to work."

"Oh . . . kay," Russ says, looking away to the excited ladies readying themselves for a high-heel sprint to the door. "But even if she's not family, it'll be thinned out by the time we get there, and the hospital probably won't even notice."

Tara scrolls up on her screen. "So, Logy says, *Helping Will's dad get the truck, we'll be back at the hospital in 20.*

Meet me there." She tucks her hair behind her ear. "You think either of them want to see Gia right now?"

"I'm sure Will's dad will understand."

"Oh, you know he does not like Gia."

As far as Will's dad is concerned, Gia ruined his son's reputation. Will was painted as a cheating boyfriend whose infidelity instigated the attack on the victim. And that—Will's dad believed—cost his son a scholarship to a power conference school, forcing him to settle for a small football program like Eastern. Whether that was true or not, Will played football because he was good at it, not because he loved it, so Eastern was no problem for him.

The excited ladies shuffle closer to the entrance. Cake-Butt looks herself over, smoothing her dress. The friend clicks on her phone, checking the time. Whoever Cake-Butt is waiting for is lucky. No girl has ever been half that excited to see Russ. He imagined it of Tara, but she's never really been thrilled by him. There might have been some flirting, sure, but Russ is entrenched in the friend zone.

"So, Logan doesn't know we're here?" Russ asks.

"No," she snaps. "And he's not going to find out. I love Logy, but if he knew . . ."

The dead crow flashes in Russ's mind. "Then what?"

She eyes him. "What do you think? He'd be mad as hell, probably never speak to me again."

"One of us should be there when Will wakes—to tell him about Gia."

She keeps typing.

"Since you know Gia," Russ says, "maybe you can hang with her, and I could go—"

"That's not going to work either."

From inside the release center, a buzzer sounds, muffled by the brick walls. The entrance door opens, and a short, husky, stiff-jawed woman struts out. Cake-Butt scurries to her, high heels clacking, and leaps up, wrapping her legs around the woman's waist. Gripping her rear, the woman pulls Cake-Butt in tight and kisses her with more tongue than a French bulldog.

Another buzzer. This time, a pale, middle-aged woman, sloppily overweight, with disheveled hair, limps out the door, wheezing. She pumps her arm triumphantly, the fat hanging from her biceps flapping as she slogs toward a dented-up Camry with a driver who's an older version of herself. The driver flicks a cigarette out her window and starts the car. The parolee waddles past the cake crew—who are meandering to their own ride—to the passenger-side door, grunting as she squeezes in and sits. The car dips, jostling the driver. No kiss, no hug. Just business as usual, as if she's being picked up from school detention. The Camry sputters off.

When the buzzer sounds again, Russ holds his breath. Tulip-Man stands, readying the flowers to his front. Stepping out from the prison is a young Asian girl, tall, petite, shiny hair pulled to one side down her chest. Tulip-Man sits. Russ keeps his breath. The girl holds a clear plastic baggie with items like lip balm, a make-up brush, and powder. She wears jeans and a white T-shirt, like the attire of the other releasees.

Tara cracks her door but then pauses, watching the girl scan each vehicle.

Tulip-Man scratches the back of his head and says something to the girl, who smiles and shakes her head gently.

"That's her, right?" Russ asks.

Tara doesn't answer, just stares.

"Tara. Is that Gia?" Russ can't remember ever seeing Gia in person. Freshman year, he had likely seen her in passing. But at that time, he wasn't friends with Will yet, or the people in his circle. He had, however, seen pictures of Gia online.

"Maybe this isn't a good idea," Tara says.

Gia sidesteps away from Tulip-Man, stands on her tiptoes, and peers at the back of the parking lot.

Slowly, Russ opens his door. As he gets out, rising above the doorframe, he waves peacefully.

Gia steps back toward Tulip-Man and whispers something to him. As Russ walks toward the prison, he looks back at Tara, her face half-hidden below the steering wheel. This must be harder for her than she expected: Gia was one of Tara's best friends, but so was Keely.

As Russ approaches, he waves again, trying to put a disarming smile on his face. "Gia, right?" he says.

She doesn't answer.

Tulip-Man stands.

"I'm Russ Burton, Will's friend." He stops over an arm's length from her.

Tulip-Man steps closer. "Is everything alright?" he asks Gia.

"What's going on?" she asks. "Where's Will?"

Russ looks back at Tara again. "Can we maybe talk by the car?"

Gia squints, trying to make out the driver.

"It's Tara," Russ says.

"Tara Saay?" She looks harder at the figure hunched in the driver's seat. "What's going on, please."

Russ sighs. "Will is in the hospital."

Her eyes widen, and she steps back.

"He was shocked in the pool."

"What?"

Behind Russ, Tara opens her door—standing, revealing herself, but keeping the door in front of her like a shield.

Gia, holding her stomach as if she just took a punch to the gut, glances at Tara and then concentrates back on Russ.

"It happened at Rando's," Russ says. "The pool light was . . . faulty or something."

"Tell me he's okay," she says, taking several steps toward the car, then stopping, waiting for an answer.

Again, Will's bloated body floats up into Russ's mind, the grayness of it, the disconnectedness. "He's in the ICU."

"Oh my God," she cries, moving faster to the car.

Tara steps out from behind the door, arms wide, receiving Gia, squeezing her, rubbing her back. They cry on contact, the sobbing muffled as their faces bury into each other's shoulders. Russ senses the connection between them.

"Can you take me to him?" Gia asks, weeping.

"They're not letting anyone see him," Tara says, a remorseful look on her face. "And they're only letting family in the waiting area."

"I have to be at the hospital. I'll talk with Will's dad."

"It's not just that. Logan's there."

The color drains from Gia's face.

"Come on," Tara says, "I have somewhere we can go."

9

Although Tara's family calls it a lake house, there is no lake. There's water, however, lots of it, what with the house being perched at the edge of Henderson Bay, another claw mark in the Puget Sound. To Russ, calling it a lake house is absurd. Humpback whales can't just wander into a lake as they do into the bay. Yet he understands the name has nothing to do with the body of water, and everything to do with the idea of a lake house: an escape.

Russ knows that Tara seldomly takes friends there, himself included. It's not a place for big parties or vacations. More than once, Tara confided in him, describing the lake house as a refuge from her mother, a highly skilled and effective socialite but a crude and ineffective nurturer, who always chose to decline going there. Tara seemed to like talking about her mom with him, perhaps because he could relate. Although she acted as if she despised her mother outright, he got the sense that she actually admired her.

Tonight, as they drive toward the lake house, through the dark, through its neighborhood with its decorative streetlamps, hexagonal glass fixtures atop black metal poles, one of the lights flickers like a candle. As Tara turns the Tesla onto the asphalt driveway, Russ finishes giving Gia the details about the party: the chicken fight, the skinny dive, the pool light, the rescue. Gia's face remains frozen, like an over-clicked computer screen.

Along both sides of the extended driveway, skinny evergreen trees, uniformly spaced, stand erect, stiff, guards saluting the arrival of royal inhabitants. The front of the lake house is unassuming, looking like a small cottage but with an attached two car garage.

Russ follows the girls inside. He knows the drill—shoes off and placed inside a cubby in the oak shoe rack. The lake house is shaped like a trapezoid, expanding outward, with an open design. A long back wall of shadeless windows overlook the deck and the beach, security lights illuminating the sand and pebbles, which from here look like faded Skittles.

The kitchen is manly but modern, like something out of *GQ* magazine. There are no feminine touches, no cute animal themes or live-laugh-love décor. The cabinets are dark, accented against white quartz counters. Cocktail glasses line the cabinet shelves, the glasses arranged by height. A consistent design scheme pervades the entire home interior: refined, free, sophisticated, rugged.

A cigar box is centered on an oversized coffee table in the living room. Art pieces burst with masculinity—old Greek guys and street art from the '90s that some would characterize as graffiti.

"Make yourself at home," Tara says, taking stock of the refrigerator's contents behind its glass door, the fridge light showing vegetables, tofu, alcohol mixes, cheeses, and an assortment of beverages. "We've got beer, wine, soda water, sparkling water . . ."

Russ's feet are gritty, his skin dried out, sunbaked. He sits on the stool at the head of the breakfast bar in the kitchen. Propping his elbows on the quartz, he puts his face into his hands and begins rubbing both eyes with his fingers, massaging them. In his mind, random images appear and disappear—Will's unmoving eyes, Tara jabbing his chest, Tulip-Man rising, Logan spitting chew.

Opening his eyes, everything is blurry, including Gia, holding her plastic baggie, pacing across the lush, dark brown rug spanning half the living room. He wonders how it must feel on her bare feet after years of walking on cement, but based on the way she steps, like her feet aren't sure where to go, the comfort of the luxury seems to have no effect.

Arms wide, Tara walks gingerly toward the distraught girl as if ready to catch her. Russ scoots to the front of the stool, allowing his toes to contact the ground. As Tara approaches her, Gia stops abruptly, surprised, as if jolted out of deep thought. She looks over the offered hug, hesitates, and leans in, only contacting her shoulders and upper chest, quickly patting Tara's back.

"Thank you for picking me up," Gia says, breaking the embrace. "I just can't believe it. I'm at a total loss here."

Tara sits on the couch facing the breakfast bar. "All we can do is wait. I'm getting updates on my phone, and I'll let you know when there's any news."

Russ stands. "You know, I think I'll take you up on that sparkling water," he says. "Y'all want one?"

Tara nods and holds up two fingers.

Russ sets all three on the coffee table, each on an oak-round coaster, then takes a seat in an armchair.

Gia sits on the couch, an empty cushion between her and Tara. She sets her baggie on the coffee table and buries her face in her hands, her long dark hair falling over her arms.

Tara cracks a cap. "You want a drink?"

"Um, not right now, thank you."

The first image that usually comes up in a search for Gia Navarro is her mugshot, her remorseful face, like that of a sad kid looking up at a parent. Russ always found himself unaffected by the seemingly photographic plea for forgiveness, because the idea of Keely Cristy stuck in the feces and piss of countless humans seemed too much to forgive, even for a face like that. Now, knowing how Will feels about Gia, Russ feels a sense of duty come over him.

"It's been so long since you've been here," Tara says. "Of course, these aren't ideal circumstances, but it's good to see you back."

Gia looks at Tara as if realizing that she is no longer in prison. Wiping her eyes, Gia examines the room, seeming to pay particular attention to the liquor cabinet, absolutely packed with an assortment of colorful labels on glass bottles. "God, it's crazy being back here, but it still feels like I'm in a nightmare." She wipes her eyes again and takes a long, slow breath as if trying to stop the flow of tears.

Gia studies a picture inside a silver frame on an oak side-table. "Does your dad still have the Bolt?" she asks, sniffing, picking up the picture and flashing it at Tara, a photograph of a yellow-striped boat.

"The Bolt baby," Tara says. "He should have never gotten rid of that one. He's got a beefed-up Bayliner now, but it's not the same."

Gia sets the picture down and puts her face back into her hands.

"Hey," Tara says, "remember those douches who wanted to race us in their dorky pink MasterCraft?"

Gia tilts her head and looks at Tara. "How could I forget. A lot was on the line."

Russ gets up and walks to the back of the side table, taking the picture frame. In the boat is Tara's dad, shirtless, barrel chested, hairy, his arm around a slightly younger version of Tara during a pink-hair phase.

"That bet was your idea, I think," Tara says, taking a sip.

Russ sets down the picture and returns to his seat.

"Well," Gia says, "the Bolt was undefeated, and you were driving, so maybe I got a little *cheeky.*"

The girls giggle, Gia's puffy eyes squeezing shut for a moment.

Russ looks back and forth at each of them, waiting for some explanation of the inside joke.

"It was a good bet," Tara says. "Those guys had to show their bright white cheeks."

Now, Russ chuckles, picturing the scene: these two hotties in a yellow-striped speed boat flexing on some cocky chumps, the girls smoking them across the water, victorious, windblown hair, pointing and laughing as the losers drop their shorts.

"The look on their faces as we blew by . . ." Gia says. "That was even better than winning the bet."

"I just remember Keely covering her eyes when they had to depants."

Russ adds a third girl to the scene: the now-dead one. And his stomach fills with anticipation.

The laughter dies off quickly, the thought of Keely lingering like a shadow.

Tara checks her phone and sets it down.

"Any news?" Russ asks.

Tara shakes her head.

Gia fans her eyes with her hand and then opens the plastic baggie on the table, picking out the lip balm.

"I gotta ask," Tara says. "What was it like in prison? I mean, you don't have to talk about it if you don't want. I'm just curious."

Gia sits up straighter. "No, it's fine. Um, it's . . . truthfully? It's insane." She glides the balm over her lips. "And everything is dirty. Not just the buildings and the yard—but all of us inmates, at least that's the way we're seen, you know."

"Really?"

"It's like we're stained and can't be cleaned. I feel bad for the people still in there."

"Yeah . . ."Tara says. "I can't imagine."

"Is the food just horrible?" Russ asks.

Tara shoots him a look as if the question is insensitive or something.

Gia leans back and wrinkles her nose. "Let's just say I never want to eat hot dogs or fish patties again."

Tara pats her own quads. "Well, then," she says, standing and marching toward the kitchen. "What would you go for right now?"

"Oh, that's okay. I'm not even hungry."

"Come on. How about a salad or something?"

"No, really."

"It's your first night."

Gia looks down at the rug. "A salad would be good, thank you."

Tara flings open the fridge and gathers romaine, cucumbers, snap peas, and mushrooms.

"You want some help?" Gia asks.

"No way, but you guys should come sit at the counter." Tara grabs a cutting board, a knife, and a strainer. She whips a dish towel over her shoulder and begins rinsing the vegetables.

Russ takes his same seat at the breakfast counter. Gia sits two seats over, resting her forearms on the quartz. A bandage pokes out of her sleeve.

"What happened to your arm?" he asks. "A shanking?" As the bad joke leaves his lips, a feeling of cringe stabs at his stomach.

Tara stops drying the vegetables and glares at him.

"Oh, that would be a good story, I wish," Gia says, checking her arm. "Actually, I fell onto a metal bench."

"Ouch," Russ says.

"I've always been clumsy, but now I fall all the time, like some old lady."

"Oh, Gia," Tara says in a sympathetic voice. "You have the same thing as your dad, don't you."

Gia nods.

"I'm sorry."

Russ wants to ask about her condition but doesn't, avoiding another silent scolding from Tara.

"I need to get a hold of him somehow," Gia says.

"Your dad?" Tara asks, slicing through the core of the onion, the blade banging on the cutting board.

"He's survived with his—our—condition for a long time. I need to know how."

Tara scoops diced onions onto her blade and dumps them into an olivewood salad bowl. She grabs a cucumber. "You know where he is?"

"I have an idea, but it's been a while since I've heard from him."

"How far from here?"

"A few hours."

Russ studies Tara's face. She seems to be calculating, probably trying to figure out how to get Gia to her dad's.

Tara rinses her hands in the sink and pats them dry on her towel. "Caesar dressing, right?" she asks, opening the fridge.

Gia smiles. "You remember."

She sets three bowls and three bottles of different dressings on the counter. "I just can't forget that time when Will ordered you ranch dressing at that steakhouse downtown, on Homecoming, I think, and he took the liberty of pouring it on for you. He was so sure that was your jam. And when you came back from the bathroom, you squinted at your bowl and then raised an eyebrow at him. I don't know why that sticks in my head."

"Oh god, what a brat I was," Gia says, holding a smile that starts to shake.

"Oh, no," Tara says, "it was cute, I didn't mean . . ."

Gia's smile crumbles, and her eyes well. "It's okay, it's not about the Homecoming dinner."

"I know."

Russ, having only been a spectator in this sad reminiscing session, grabs the ranch, clears his throat, and says, "Will is a Viking."

Both girls look at him with tilted heads, then look at each other.

"He's tough, like a Viking, is what I mean."

"Right," Tara says. "Will is as tough as they come."

Gia straightens. "Let me guess, he told you he *is* part Viking, didn't he?"

"Uh, yeah," Russ says, capping the dressing. "He has lineage to the Vikings, or something like that."

Gia titters. "That guy. It's one thing to tell people you have Norwegian family, but to say you're a Viking . . . he's something else." She shakes her head, as if shaking away the thought of crying again.

Tara grabs the Caesar dressing. "All hail Will Caesar," she says, holding the bottle high, pouring a glug onto the heap of vegetables.

Gia chuckles.

"Julius Caesar was Roman," Russ says. "Not a Viking."

"It's close enough, Russell. And just like the Vikings, Caesar was a bad ass. Like Will. So, there you go. Now, pass the pepper, would you."

In a glass holder, on his end of the breakfast counter, there are two stainless-steel salt and pepper shakers. As he plucks out the pepper, the shaker slips, banging down onto the quartz, rolling for the edge. Russ times the drop, but fumbles, the shaker banging down onto the tile.

"Real smooth, Russell," Tara says, giggling.

"Sorry," he says, bending down. As he grabs the shaker, pretending not to notice the spilled pepper grounds, he notices a band around Gia's ankle. "They're tracking you?" he asks, rising up, bumping his head on the counter.

"You, okay?" Gia asks, covering her mouth to stop from laughing.

"Yeah, yeah, I'm fine. I'm on a roll, I guess." Russ passes the pepper to Tara.

Gia peers down at her ankle. "It's a condition of my release, unfortunately. This thing sucks. It's like wearing a rubber ducky wrapped around my leg.

"Damn," Russ says.

"It makes the State of Washington my new prison. If I go out of state, I'll be back in my old cell."

She jabs her salad and raises the fork, skewered with a medley of cool vegetables. She holds it out in front, examining it as if it were a glass of wine, as if delighting in the colors, the cleanliness, the crisp edges. She smiles at Tara and takes a bite.

Tara and Russ join her, crunching, both keeping their gaze on Gia—her eyes are closed as she chews softly.

"So, Russ," Gia says, "Will told me you got valedictorian?" She jabs another forkful.

"Uh, yeah . . ." Russ says, the spanking steaming back into his mind for the first time in hours. "I always thought it'd feel different though."

"Yeah?"

"I'm not sure how to explain it . . ."

"I know what you mean," Tara says. "It's the same for me and UCLA. I've imagined it forever and now that I'm actually going, it feels like business-as-usual or something. I just hate that I have to go so soon."

"No way you're going tomorrow, right?" Russ says.

On the counter, Tara's phone lights up. As she reads the message, Gia and Russ remain still.

"Okay, okay," Tara says, "Will is doing better. They have him in an induced coma, but he's stable."

Gia stands, looking ready to leave right then.

Tara sets her phone face down. "It's good news, but he's still in ICU, so no visitors."

Gia paces behind her chair. "He's in an induced coma?"

"He's stable though," Tara says.

"I just can't help but think . . . what are the chances, you know, that the faulty pool light comes on right as he dives in?"

"I know. It really could have been any of us, or all of us." Tara brings her bowl to the sink. She flips a switch on the wall and rinses the remains, a half bowl of salad, into the whirling garbage disposal.

The grinding of the disposal causes Russ to imagine twenty kids in the pool, groaning, screaming, electrified. It could have been a massacre, all their friends, even Russ and Tara. But maybe Will being the only one was no accident. The dead crow flashes in Russ's mind.

"I really hate that I have to leave in the morning," Tara says.

"Actually?" Russ asks. "You're still going to LA?"

"I can't sign my lease remotely. I'll be back in a couple days. I'm guessing they'll let visitors in by then. But you guys can stay here however long you want."

Did she just say *you guys*? As if Russ needs to stay here.

"You'll take care of Gia, right Russ?"

"Oh, he doesn't have to—"

"Nonsense," Tara says, cutting her off. "This is Will Bayman's best friend. "Of course he has your back."

"What about . . ." Russ starts. "What about your dad?"

"He'll be cool with it. Don't worry, I'll talk to him. Our Jeep is in the garage, and the keys are right here," she says, grabbing a key fob from a kitchen drawer. "Russel, you take care of your best friend's girl. Wherever she needs to go . . . go. Just bring the Jeep back when you're done."

Russ cracks his knuckles. He hates it when she calls him Russell, especially as she bosses him around.

"There's two guest bedrooms," Tara says. "Have your pick. And help yourselves to anything. Gia, there's a ton of clothes in my room. And Russ, my dad has pretty good style. He won't mind if you borrow something."

10

Logan hasn't slept, but he's not tired. A small amount of adrenalin lingers in his bloodstream, like Will's blood still lingering in the pool. When Logan dragged him out of the water—perhaps a little earlier than he should have—blood dripped from a hole in Will's arm where the electricity blew out of his body. Hospital staff notified the family of the exit wound, where muscle tissue, fat, and bone fragments flew from Will's tricep, leaving a gap the size of a golf ball. The family didn't share this detail with many. But they did share it with Logan, perhaps because he rescued Will, as if he were a guardian angel—instead of a demon.

For some reason, maybe because the family trusted him, Logan didn't tell anyone about the exit wound, even Tara. Logan did, however, text Tara about Will's general condition, him being in an induced coma but stable. Oddly, Tara, someone who usually texts back quickly, still hasn't responded.

Sitting in his truck, Logan flips down his visor, shading his eyes from the morning sunlight slicing through a break in the sheet of gray clouds. His eyes are now shaded, but the stubble on his face stays lit, as does his bulging lip, tobacco snuff jammed into his bottom gum.

Next to his truck is a parking meter, a useless machine on Sundays when parking is free. Below the meter, the curb is gnarled, and a trail of water trickles along the gutter to a storm drain where a wet receipt clings to a metal grate. From this parking spot, he has a perfect view of the entrance to Tara's father's office building.

Logan checks for pedestrians before spitting a stream of black saliva out his window and into the gutter. He's still in his swim shorts, but the pool light remote is no longer in his pocket. Last night, on his way to the hospital, he slipped it out of his truck window, onto the freeway, for the vehicles behind him to destroy.

The slice of sun lasts for only a few seconds. Clouds merge and blend, blocking out the direct light, leaving the city coated in dullness. Skyscrapers lean over the truck's foggy windshield as raindrops start to sprinkle the glass. For a weekend morning, downtown is bustling. Coffee cups and cell phones lead the way for umbrella-carrying weekend-workers, while bottles wrapped with damp paper bags lead the way for the homeless. Buses and delivery vans pass restaurant patrons eating breakfast outdoors, under canopies, steam rising off their eggs.

Logan counts two coffee shops and seven recycling bins. He has always loved numbers, counting crops, counting the freckles on Keely's arms and back while they lay together at the farm. His favorite freckle was in the shape of a crescent on her back, freckle number six below her neckline. If it had been up to Logan, he would have spent every weekend at the farm with Keely, but she, despite being a tad shy, liked the social scene and the parties and feared missing out, something Logan never understood. Even so, Logan would take her out at her request. And although he would never dance, he loved to watch her move to the beat.

After her first drink, she would start bouncing around the party. By drink number three, she would be right next to the speakers, her movements growing bigger, freer. And once Tara and Gia joined her, all three would dance like nothing mattered. Everyone else would watch, including Logan and Will, their girlfriends both in the mix. But Will didn't always seem to have his focus on his own girlfriend.

Out of the three girls, Gia was broadly considered the prettiest: her hair was silky, raven-black, long like her slender, model-typical body. But Keely was beautiful too, and on a deeper level. She was innocent, sweet, gentle. They were best friends, probably closer to each other than either was to Tara, until something went wrong. Gia sensed something; perhaps it started with Will's wandering eye. There were rumors: Will and Keely were hooking up.

On the seat next to Logan, there's a gym bag and two cell phones. He takes the one with a black case and dials 988.

"Northwest Suicide and Crisis Lifeline, my name is Chad and with whom do I have the pleasure of speaking?"

Logan clears his throat and says, "Larry Washington."

"Good morning, Mr. Washington. I'm glad you called. May I call you Larry?""First off, I want you to know that I'm not sad. I'm not one of those 'poor me' kind of guys."

"Well, we all get sad sometimes, but before we continue, can I ask if you're in a safe place?"

Chad sounds like he's in his early twenties, probably a do-gooder, probably a redhead with one of those creepy thin red goatees, probably somewhat fresh out of training. "Yes, Chad, and just so you know, I won't be offing myself just yet, so you don't have to worry about that."

With the cadence of someone reading, Chad asks, "Are you having thoughts about harming yourself or taking your own life?"

"Don't even tell me you're using a cheat sheet."

"A cheat sheet? No, of course not. I mean, we keep reference materials but nothing that would be considered cheating."

"I'm a little surprised. The woman I spoke to last time was very unscripted, very nurturing."

"Oh, would you feel more comfortable talking to someone else, a woman perhaps?"

"You're not trying to ditch me, right? What does your cheat sheet say about ditching callers?"

"I would never ditch a caller, Mr. Washington—I was only trying to be accommodating."

Logan examines a Tesla driving by, but it's not the color he's looking for. "Do you believe in God, Chad?"

Chad hesitates.

Logan huffs at the thought of this guy perusing a list of responses. "Forget the cheat sheet."

"My personal beliefs aren't something I can discuss, but if you'd like to talk about yours, I'm here to listen."

"Okay, Chad, if you read one more line of bullshit from that sheet . . ."

"I'm sorry, Mr. Washington, I don't want to say the wrong thing here. Perhaps I should get my supervisor."

"I don't want to talk to your supervisor, Chad. I want to know what you think."

"What was the question again, sorry."

"Do you, Mr. Chad, believe in God?"

Chad takes a deep breath and probably closes his eyes. "I . . . I go back and forth."

"Ah. A refreshing answer. Most people won't admit that out loud. They have their doubts, but when it comes to saying whether they believe, they almost always say yes. And do you know why they say yes, Chad?"

"No, sir, I don't."

"Just in case. That's why." Logan spits out the window. "Just in case God is real. If they admit doubt, they're subject to a good ass-whooping by the almighty."

"How about you, Mr. Washington, do you believe?"

Logan chuckles. "When I was a kid, I had Bible studies every Sunday, like clockwork. The best part was the animal crackers. Everything else sucked. I had to sit there listening to all these stories that no honest, rational person would ever believe, or so I thought. And the rules were mostly crazy too. Except for some, of course. I mean, I get that murder goes without saying, except for the exceptions. But why isn't taking your own life an exception? Is that really murder? Is it really a sin?"

"A priest might know that one, but a better question might be, why waste the life you have? Whether God exists or not, you're alive, and you can choose to live it out, see what happens, do something that matters to you."

"Alright, Chad, your best answer today. But here's the thing, if all the people you care about are gone, and when everything worth doing is done, why stay around?"

"Because you might find someone who you care about, and you might find something worth doing."

Logan doesn't answer. Outside, a construction flagger smokes a cigarette in the sprinkling rain, holding the cigarette in her lips, protecting it under her jacket's hood. The car she's stopping is a Tesla, the right color.

"Mr. Washington, are you still there?"

Logan can see now that the driver is Tara. "Chad . . ."

"Yes, sir."

"You should shave your goatee."

"I don't have a—"

Logan ends the call and waits until Tara parks her car. When she starts for the entrance, Logan gets out of his truck and hustles up the sidewalk. At the crosswalk, he waits for traffic to pass, the vehicles sloshing water under their tires, raindrops pattering his cowboy hat.

"Tara," he shouts, jogging through an opening in traffic despite the red hand telling him not to cross. He sprints up the flight of stairs toward the covered entrance.

As she grabs a handle on one of three glass double doors, Logan calls for her again.

She turns, and her eyes widen. "Logan?" She keeps a grip on the handle.

"Sorry," he says, approaching, catching his breath, "I didn't mean to scare you."

The tightness of Tara's face doesn't match the looseness of her relaxed-fit athleisure clothing, boyfriend-style sweatpants, and zip-up sweater. "What are you doing here?" Tara asks. "Is it Will? Is he worse?"

"No, nothing's changed." He holds up a cell phone in an orange case.

"Okay," she says, sounding uncertain. "What's up with the phone?"

"It's Russ's. He left it in Will's truck. I thought you might know where he is."

"Why didn't you just text me?"

"My phone's dead, for one thing, but I also wanted to say goodbye."

She lets the door go. "What do you mean? Are you going somewhere?"

"What? No, you are."

"Oh, right. I'll be back in just a couple of days. Hopefully, they let Will out of the coma, and I can see him."

Tara thinks for a second. "Oh good, you got my texts."

"I saw them this morning. I woke up late—no surprise. I haven't had time to text anyone back."

"Any idea where Russ might be?"

"Uh, no. Wasn't he at the hospital last night?"

"He wasn't. Isn't that weird? Will's best friend, not even there."

Tara thinks for a second. "You said they weren't allowing visitors. Maybe he stayed home."

"How would Russ know?" Logan wiggles Russ's phone.

Tara shrugs her shoulders. "You'll have to ask him."

"You two left together, from the party, right? That's why I thought you might know where he is."

"We did. I dropped him off at his house." She checks the time on her phone. "Shit, Logy, I've got to—"

"Huh, weird. Well, I'll swing back by there."

"You already checked?"

"No one was home. It was like 6 a.m. I rang the doorbell three or four times."

Tara clicks on her phone again. "I really have to go."

"Yeah, okay," Logan says, opening his arms for a hug. "Well, you travel safe."

Reluctantly, she lets go of the door handle. She leans in, pats him on the back near his shoulder, and backs away. "I'll see you in a few days. Let me know if you hear anything about Will, okay." She opens the door and seems to force a smile.

"Yeah," he says, taking a step back. "Hey, just one more thing. Last night, at the hospital, I was thinking about Will and all the good times . . ." He glances down and shakes his head, as if to fight back tears. "You remember that time we had the bonfire on the beach, just a few of us, and Will was beating his chest around it like a caveman."

"I do remember that."

"Where the hell were we?" "My dad's lake house—" Her face goes long. "Or was it? I don't remember. No . . . actually, I think it was somewhere else."

"Henderson Bay, right?"

"Uh, I'm not sure."

"You don't know where your dad's lake house is?"

"Of course, but I'm just not sure we were there."

"Okay. Well, it doesn't matter. I'll see you soon." Logan smiles and turns away.

11

When Russ wakes, he finds everything under his damp towel is shriveled like a raisin.

He took a shower before bed, turning up the water so hot it bordered on being painful. He dried himself with the fluffiest, thickest towel he'd ever used. Wrapping it around his waist, Russ sat on the edge of the bed, his limbs limp, his mind tangled with an array of thoughts and images: being spanked publicly (and on video), Will in a coma, Gia coming out of prison, Tara ready to fly off, Logan's (possible) cruel intentions. He lay back on the bed for just a second, for just a quick break, sinking into the memory foam, swearing to himself he'd get up in just a minute to grab some clothes and brush his teeth.

Now, a few hours later, in this unfamiliar room, the second/junior guest bedroom of the lake house, where the morning light filters through beige curtains, the thick towel still wet, everything under it having gone cold during the night. He rolls out of bed and pushes the heavy towel down off his body. It thuds on the carpet as he staggers for the en suite bathroom, rubbing an eye, glancing back at the bed and the wet spot the towel left on the feather-filled comforter, reminding him of the wet spot left on the concrete after the paramedics took Will.

In the mirror above the pedestal sink, he shows his teeth, sliding his tongue along his slimy front row, the remnants of salad dressing and a bit of lettuce pasted on the enamel. Although his mouth is dirty, his body is clean and smells of pineapple body wash. He dabs toothpaste on his finger and rubs it along his gumline, circling to the backsides. His swim trunks dangle over the shower door. The elastic waistband has three ridges, matching the three grooves in the skin around Russ's waist. Like the memory foam of the mattress, the grooves have nearly returned to their original shape. He snatches the shorts off the shower and walks back into the bedroom.

As he prepares to slip them back on, and bear the redeepening of the grooves, he notices folded clothes on the dresser and a note sticking out from the bottom of a pair of black boxer-briefs.

Russell,
These are my dad's but straight out of the package. They might be a little big so don't let your new panties bunch. Haha. Take care of Gia. See you soon!
- Tara

Russ smiles at the exclamation point. He tosses the swim shorts onto the bed and sniffs the boxer-briefs, confirming the new-clothes smell. He slips them on and turns sideways, checking the fit in the dresser's mirror. Not bad. Maybe he's meatier than Tara thinks. He puts on a pair of olive-green golf shorts and a black polo, snug on his torso. He looks himself over: it's not exactly his style, but he looks mature, a tad sophisticated, like a stockbroker in the casual.

He peeks through the side of the curtains, to the empty driveway. The Tesla is gone. Behind him, a clock ticks. Until now, he hasn't noticed the sound—surprising considering how loud it clanks. He noticed the clock, of course, the extra-large-pizza-sized wall decoration with gold roman numerals and brass gears at its center. Since fourth grade, Russ has hated Roman numerals, a system that only slows the process, forcing a translation to modern numbers. How dumb. It's not as if Roman numerals make clock time more important or give Super Bowls more significance, nor do they give suffixes prestige (Harry Balls III could just be Harry Balls the Third).

The ticking clock triggers something in Russ: a flood of dread. The array of thoughts and images begins pulsating through his mind again. He grabs a remote off the dresser and sits at the foot of the bed across from a smart TV. As he scrolls through its apps, he finds a web browser and navigates to his social media. Holding his breath, he signs in, expecting an update on Will. There's no bad news, just prayers and well wishes.

Surprisingly, he also finds people are pissed at the FitzRoys, calling them broke-asses and demanding they hire some real contractors. Russ navigates to Will's father's page. There's his picture: Big Bill Bayman. He posted an update an hour ago—Will is still in the ICU, in critical but stable condition. Bill must wonder where Russ has been.

Russ sends him a message:

Bill, I know there were too many people at the hospital last night. Is it okay for me to come down now?

Russ hopes for a quick reply but doesn't get one.

If he goes to the hospital, Gia would have to stay behind, which would suck, but maybe Russ brings back good news—maybe Will wakes, maybe Russ gets to tell him that Gia is in a safe place and waiting.

He opens up a new tab and scrolls through other feeds to see what people are saying about Will, but also checking—and hoping—no one is talking about what happened at graduation. Now that Will is everyone's focus, he was almost expecting nothing about the speech, but despite Will's tragic accident, despite Will being hospitalized, hanging on to life in a coma, people are still talking about Russ—perhaps even more so—with new jokes, new memes, new humiliation.

There's a link to a new video. He hesitates, then clicks.

On the screen—and on countless other screens, he knows—there he is: Red-Butt Russ, his face revealed unmistakably, his grimace, his pleading for the old man to stop. Much closer and clearer than the other video he saw. This one was taken from the front row.

The number of views is sickening, and Russ feels literally sick to his stomach. He clicks back to his home page, ridding the screen of the ridicule. As he heads for the bathroom—wanting to be near the toilet should he actually puke—Russ grows lightheaded and braces his palms against the dresser. His body is sweaty, shaky.

Focusing on his breath, he shuts his eyes and waits.

It only takes a few minutes for his body to settle. When he opens his eyes, he's staring at Tara's note, staring directly at the exclamation point.

He has the urge to call Will, but since he can't, he considers reaching out to Morgan, Russ's mom. That almost always goes bad, of course. She's constantly mad about something. Right now, it's the graduation speech, which clearly, she should have seen in person. If she had, things may have gone totally different. Would Russ have made the verbal attack on Eckspun with his mom right there? Not likely.

Realizing she still might not know of Will's accident, he navigates to her page. There's her picture: Morgan Burton, in yoga gear, next to her boyfriend, Jeremiah the Bullfrog—emphasis on the bull. He's a liar and a cheat. Behind them is a Mexican sunrise. Morgan and the Bullfrog are in some kind of yoga prayer pose. A caption at the bottom of the picture reads, *Our hearts and prayers go out to the Baymans.*

So, she already heard, and she hasn't sent one message to Russ? No simple DM? Or maybe she texted him—duh—but of course he doesn't have his phone.

The cursor blinks under *Send Morgan a Message.* Morgan is not his mom's real name, but it's the name she prefers people call her, and that goes for Russ too. To most young children, it's difficult to comprehend their mothers having names other than Mom, but Russ learned early, required to call her Morgan for as long as he could remember. That said, there were certain situations where he did have to call her Mom—primarily when other adults were around, excluding boyfriends.

Her real name is Martha, a name she despises, a name she associates with old women, wrinkled and stinky. Being called Mom, however, is just as bad, if not worse. Moms aren't glamorous or full of adventure. The name Morgan is apparently modern, trendy, fashionable.

Many of Russ's childhood memories surround his mom's great efforts to cultivate her beauty, always plucking, primping, brushing, blushing, lining, while little Russ tried his best to do things on his own without disturbing her, like trying not to spill milk while making himself cereal for dinner. As Morgan aged, it took even more work and effort to upkeep her desired look, but it was a losing game, age winning round after round. As a result, Morgan became frightened and angry. Her key asset was fading, and trips out of the country for certain procedures, funded by her boyfriend(s), became frequent.

Russ sends her a message:

Hi Morgan, it looks like you heard about Will's accident. Seeing him unconscious on the concrete, I wasn't sure he was going to make it. It was scary. He's stable now but still in a coma. I don't have my phone. DM me if you need anything and I'll reply as soon as I can.

Sometimes Russ wonders why she kept her pregnancy. She's admitted that Russ's father, who she apparently only knew by his first name, Nate, wanted her to get an abortion. Morgan also has admitted she didn't want a baby but kept the fetus because it was the Catholic thing to do. She's told Russ all this as if honesty is really the best policy.

The TV dings loud with a notification.

Message from Morgan:

Russell, Will is strong, he'll be fine. Listen, me and Jeremiah have been talking a lot, and we both agree, and I know the timing isn't ideal, but now that you are done with school it's time for you to find your own place. We'll be in Mexico for a few more weeks. That should be enough time for you to find at least a temporary living arrangement. Let me know if you hear more about Will. Cheers.

Russ springs to his feet. Jeremiah agrees? Cheers? Unbelievable. Russ almost slams the remote to the floor like he'll do with video game controllers after getting a game-over. Move out in just a few weeks? And what, move into a shelter or something? As if Russ can find a place and move out that fast, as if his best friend isn't in a coma, as if he isn't all over social media getting spanked. Unbelievable.

Of course, Russ wants out of Morgan's house anyway, but he planned to establish his securities trading firm first. Now he'll have to focus on finding a place to live, without any means. It's not like he can just move in with a friend. His only real friend is in a coma.

He's raging, a sign he should write something in his journal, a practice J-Jack convinced him to start about a year ago. His mentor described it as the best way to regulate emotions and spur creative thought. Russ searches for My Journaling App, clicks, signs in, and begins to write.

My Journaling App - Entry #98:

When you're a small kid you wonder if adults—the ones who can't stand kids—forget they were once kids themselves. As you get older, you realize that perhaps it's not just kids they hate, it's specific people, regardless of their age.

Russ leaves the room and makes his way to the kitchen. Gia is outside the sliding glass door, sitting on a patio chair, her bare feet off the wooden deck and flat on her seat. Her hair is wet and brushed. Her oversized T-shirt is tented over her knees, covering her bare legs, which jet out of jean shorts. The ankle monitor sticks out the bottom of the shirt.

Russ slides the door open. On the patio table, next to a bowl of assorted berries, two half-eaten strawberries soak into a napkin. The air is cool and misty, and fine water droplets tickle his nostrils.

"So, I guess Tara really left," Russ says, clearing his throat as he slides the screen door shut behind him.

The deck appears gray and weathered, but it's new, a rustic-coastal design. Instead of guardrails, plexiglass lines the perimeter, maximizing the view.

Gia half smiles. "Yeah, you never know with her." She looks like she's ruminating for a few seconds. "She surprised me, though, by showing up last night. I would have never expected it."

Russ sits at the table. They stare out at the blend of water and mist, the separation between bay and sky indistinguishable.

"You sleep okay?" Russ asks.

"I'm not totally sure I slept. You ever have that? You think you did, but maybe didn't go all the way to sleep or something?"

Russ nods. "It's probably that memory foam. I don't like it."

"Hmm . . . maybe I'm not used to a soft bed yet."

Russ imagines how she's slept in prison: a hard and dirty mattress on a metal rack, among criminals, with prison doors clanking shut before lights-out.

"It must be surreal being free," Russ says.

"Free? I don't feel any different." She stares out at the bay. "Maybe worse, actually."

Russ shifts in his seat. "Well, it makes sense though, right? With Will being in the hospital and everything."

She looks down at her fingers, wiggling them as if trying to restore feeling.

Russ rubs his palms across his shorts. "I was thinking about going to the hospital."

"Are they letting visitors see him?"

"Not yet, but he's stable. I just feel like I should go by, you know? I messaged Will's dad."

"And?"

"He hasn't responded yet. Do you think he'll be cool with us—"

"No. Not us. Not me. Bill would flip out if I walked in there." She wheezes as she finishes speaking.

Russ reaches for the fruit bowl, then pauses. "You mind?"

She shakes her head.

He brings a strawberry to his mouth. "It just feels weird not being at the hospital." He takes a bite, the juice running over his tongue and mixing with the aftertaste of toothpaste.

Gia takes a deliberate deep breath and closes her eyes.

Russ tosses the butt of the strawberry on the napkin. "You okay?" he asks, still chewing, scooting to the edge of his chair.

She nods. "It gets worse when I'm stressed."

"What?"

"My condition," she says. "It's not good right now." She keeps her eyes closed, laboring, mildly panting.

Russ stands. "What should I do?"

She waves him off.

Last night, Gia showed no indication of being ill or struggling with any disorder. But it has crossed Russ's mind, what with Will having mentioned her condition at the Coop. It was odd that Will even mentioned Gia. He's hardly ever said a word about her, maybe two or three times max in the last year since Russ returned from Texas with Morgan, leaving behind Glenn the Great—perhaps her scariest boyfriend.

Whenever Will accidently mentioned Gia, he'd quickly change the subject. So, Russ learned very little about her or their history. Will had to know, however, that Russ looked her up. There was so much written on the web about it, the jealous girlfriend forcing her rival—her former best friend—into a holding tank of human waste.

Nonetheless, Russ never asked Will about it, and Will never volunteered to fill him in.

Gia's breath constricts to a harsher wheeze, and her face strains as if she's choking. Russ steps close. Gia holds up her hand, motioning for him to give her space.

As he steps back, she looks him in the eye.

"It's water?" she says.

"You want water?" Russ starts for the screen door. "Hold on, I'll—"

"Everything is water . . ." she says, as her focus drifts away from Russ, into nothing.

12

Russ can't tell if Gia's breathing. He lowers his face to hers, holding his own breath, listening, waiting. Finally, air drifts from her nose to his cheek. He steps back, examining her, trying to determine if she's alright. But no reasonable person could think she's okay. She's not even blinking.

Through a break in the mist, the sun hits her eyes, beating on the darks of her exposed irises. For a moment, the gleaming gold flecks in the brown of them mesmerize Russ. Because he can't stomach shutting her eyelids, like one would do to a dead person, he turns her chair instead, dragging it in a half circle until she's facing the door.

He has no phone. No way to call an ambulance. Maybe he could DM someone for help. Shaking her shoulder, Russ pleads for Gia to wake up. But she just stares, blankly. He paces. He could DM Sandra?

Russ swipes the screen door open, sending it banging against the frame. As he steps inside, Gia gasps as if she's been trapped under water and is now breaking through the surface, gulping air.

She groans. "Where are you going?"

"It'll be okay—I'm going to get an ambulance."

She motions for him to come back. "You should sit," she says, speaking low, like she has a headache. "An ambulance won't do any good."

"Shouldn't they at least check you out?"

She half grins. "That's all they can do, just check. They can't fix me."

"Are you sure you don't want—"

"I'm sure. Can you help me turn around?"

Carefully, Russ starts dragging her chair back the other way, toward the bay. As the chair scrapes along the deck, vibrating, Gia winces. "Let me get up," she says. She stands, wobbling, feeble like an old woman, grabbing Russ's arm to steady herself. "Thank you, young man."

As she looks up at him, Russ becomes flush. Her face is captivating, her skin supple, gentle.

"Can you adjust my chair now?" she asks, trying to keep her legs steady.

"Yeah, yeah, you got a hold of me, right?"

"It sure looks like it," she says.

Russ uses his free hand to reposition the chair. Keeping her grip on him, she sits back down.

Russ takes his seat too, his insides shaking, adrenaline still pumping. "You were passed out or something."

"I had an episode. A small one," she says, her tongue sounding sticky. "Can you hand me that juice."

Lunging for the glass of orange juice next to the fruit bowl, he bumps into the table.

"Easy," she says, "I'm fine."

Her body appears weak, unsteady. With deliberate concentration, she tips the glass, letting orange juice slide into her mouth. Reminded of the dry mouth he had during his valedictorian speech, Russ grabs a bottle of water and drinks. His speech—how horrible. People are watching him right now, across the internet, watching him look like a weak little boy.

Gia closes her eyes and remains quiet for a full minute. "When it happens," she says. "My episodes, I mean—it's like I'm aware but I'm not, like I'm dreaming, but I'm still in reality. It's hard to explain. Sometimes it lasts hours."

Russ rubs his stomach, the adrenaline taking a toll on his gut. "You just snap out of it?"

"I don't know how it happens. It just—"

She winces and squeezes the sides of her head.

Russ looks off into the bay, not wanting to stare as she focuses on relieving her pain.

There must be millions of organisms under the surface of the water. He has often wished he could be other creatures or things, wondering now how great it would be to be the bay itself—to exist and matter but without problems or suffering.

The clouds thicken, darkening the sky. In the distance, to the north, he sees a single sunbeam, but it's snuffed out quickly.

"It'll happen again," Gia says, "at some point." She folds her legs against her body and wraps her arms around her knees. "The long ones can go on and on, even for days. There's nothing they can do. Hospitals are a waste of time. They just test and test and find no answers. I've been on everything, every steroid, plasma exchanges—"

She winces, flashing with pain again.

"They've tried everything," she continues, "but they finally gave up and just let me out of prison."

How could someone so young, someone who looks so healthy, be so sick? She's like one of those painted eggs—delicate, exquisite, but rotting from the inside.

After a few more minutes, the muscles in Gia's face ease, and the aftershocks of her episode seem to be gone.

"Did Will tell you about my condition?" she asks.

Russ shifts in his chair. "Well, actually, until yesterday, he never told me much about . . . anything. I didn't know you guys were even seeing each other."

"I made him keep quiet. Easier . . . safer that way."

Russ nods, not exactly sure what she means but not wanting to question it. "So . . . what's it called? Your condition."

"Doon's Disease." She takes another drink. "My dad has the first recorded case. Other people have had similar auto-immune diseases, but none like ours, the way it attacks the brain stem and organs. It's so aggressive."

"Dunes?"

"D-O-O-N. It's my dad's name. It's a weird name, I know. It started as a nickname, like sand dune, and then he legally changed it. The last time I saw him, he was doing pretty good, he looked improved. We didn't talk about his condition, but yeah, he looked okay. That was before my plea deal."

"Are you saying he's found a way to get better?"

She shrugs. "I hope so. He's been searching for a cure since he started getting symptoms, just before I was born. He's dedicated his life to it. And somehow, he's survived. Either his efforts have paid off or his condition isn't as hostile as mine."

Along with an upset stomach—a side effect of his adrenaline—guilt pings in Russ's gut: He may have made it sound as if he knew nothing of Will's and Gia's history, but there was one thing Will let slip when he was drunk. He went on about Gia's family: her dad being a crazy neo-hippie with mental problems, and her mother being a deadbeat who ran out on them to Korea. As a baby, Gia was placed in the care of her Auntie Yun, her mother's sister, a real pest. They called her the Fire Ant for stinging Gia with a belt for even minor offenses, even as a teenager, when Will was around. One day—at least the way Will told it, and Russ had no reason not to believe him—Will took the belt from the Fire Ant and gave the woman a single lashing, over her jeans, although not as hard as he could have. After that, Gia was never hit again.

"My dad is probably still staying along the Skagit River," Gia says, "across the Canadian border."

"You're not sure though?" Russ asks. His chest is sweaty, and he fidgets in his chair.

"No, I'm not. He wrote to me from there a few times in prison. But it's been like nine months since I heard from him. I don't always get his mail, though." She lays her head back on the top of the backrest, gazing into the dense clouds. "I sent him a letter a couple weeks ago, letting him know of my release, and finally telling him about my condition, but who knows if he got it."

Russ leans forward in his chair. "Wait, so your dad doesn't know you have the disease?"

She shakes her head.

"Why wouldn't you—"

"I was worried he might come down here, into Washington, to sneak me in some plant extract or concoction. He's got a warrant."

Russ wants to ask about the charge but decides not to.

Gia giggles. "You probably think we're a bunch of criminals—a wanted man and his felon daughter. It's not like that. The police searched his home—he wasn't there, thank God—and they found a variety of mushrooms he was growing, including illegal ones."

"Damn," Russ says. He thinks about all of this for a second. Her last resort is her Dad, and he may or may not be along the Skagit—a few hours from here, as she'd mentioned the night before. Maybe he could get her there. But what if Doon is nowhere to be found? Then what? "I take it you don't have his cell number?""He lives off the grid. He's paranoid. And people have always found him suspicious. The few memories I have of him as a kid, people would look at us sideways, a bushy, dirty white Italian guy with a tiny Asian kid."

From the bay, a breeze cools Russ's body. "It's really your only play, trying to find him."

"It's all I got. But once I cross the border," Gia says, "I've violated my parole. I'm actually supposed to meet with my PO today."

"You want me to drive you? Tara said we could use the Jeep."

Gia brushes her hair behind her ear, exposing it, as if to signal to Russ she hopes to hear him say something different, that he'll help her get to where she really needs to go. He knows she can't do this by herself. If she has an episode while driving, it's all for naught, and someone else could get hurt.

"On second thought," Russ says, "how about a ride to the Skagit?"

Her face beams, and she flashes a full smile. "That would mean so much to me."

The legal term "aiding and abetting" flashes through Russ's mind. "Wait, what about the tracker?" He points to her ankle.

"It's just rubber. It cuts easy."

"Won't they know—"

"These things malfunction all the time. And almost no one checks in on them. That's according to experienced convicts, people I met inside. The state actually saves money when ankle monitors are cut—there's less labor and maintenance."

Another issue slides across his mind. "What about Will?"

"When he wakes, you tell him I'm waiting for him."

Russ leans over in between his knees, staring at the deck. He could drop her off and go see Will and figure out what to do about his living situation. On top of that, he would be coming through for Tara.

"Okay, how far is it exactly?"

"Three hours to Diablo Lake."

"Lake? I thought he's on a river."

"The river is damned in two spots, making two lakes. We drive to Diablo, take a ferry across, and then take a water taxi up Ross Lake. That's where we can access his cabin along the river.

Russ gathers himself. "This sounds more like an expedition than a ride."

"It's not too bad, it'll probably take us four hours total or so."

Russ does the math in his head. If they leave now, it's possible he could get back late tonight. "Let's do it," he says.

She tries to stand to hug him, but she nearly loses her balance.

"Don't worry about it," Russ says, getting up to help her sit back down.

As they both settle, one more concern drops into his mind.

"Can I ask you something?" Russ asks. "What did you mean when you said it was safer to keep it quiet about you and Will seeing each other?"

She leans back against her chair. "A couple things. One, if people knew, if the internet knew, that Will was still seeing me, he'd be excoriated. But more importantly, it was to keep Logan at a distance."

"Yeah?"

"He's a psycho. But we can't prove it."

"You think he did this to Will?"

She nods.

"We should tell the cops."

"Tell them what?"

Inside, from down the hall, in the second guest bedroom, the TV dings with a notification.

"That might be Will's dad," Russ says, standing up. "Maybe Will is out of ICU."

As he walks down the hallway slowly, Gia holding his shoulder behind him, Russ's mind is consumed with the idea that Logan is responsible. How could Logan have set that up? It seems impossible. But something isn't right. Even Will mentioned being concerned, telling Russ about the dead crow on his truck.

Russ grabs the remote off the bed and opens the message.

Message from Bill Bayman:

It's with a heavy and saddened heart that I write to inform everyone of Will's passing. A few hours ago, the Lord took our beautiful boy, who had grown into a fine young man that any father would be proud of, to a better place than this. Rest in peace my son. We love you so much.

13

Backing away, as if the screen is a threat, Gia crashes into the dresser. The mirror shakes, warping the reflection.

"Read it again," Gia says, panting. "He's stable. You said he was stable."

Russ has read the message twice to himself already, but he reads it again, this time out loud.

He starts, but he can't read past "the Lord took."

Numb, he sits on the bed. The remote falls, thudding on the floor, batteries springing out the back. Russ feels for his phone, but it's not there, of course. And even if he did have his phone, it wouldn't matter; the only person he ever really calls is Will.

Reality seeps in. Will Bayman is gone. His life effaced. His giant, dead body—if it hasn't been already—will be stuffed into a giant metal drawer. He'll be temporarily preserved, but ultimately his beast of a form will just rot away or be completely incinerated. His voice, his laugh, his friendship—the only true friendship Russ ever had—are gone forever.

Russ's numbness grows heavier, as if his body is being buried in sand.

Gia slides down the face of the dresser. As she sinks to the floor, she yelps, then wheezes like an old woman. Her face strains like someone in a horror movie who's about to be stabbed. Her gaze drifts off. She's not blinking.

Russ jumps up. "No, no, Gia, don't pass out on me now..." He kneels beside her, his palms on his forehead, his fingers pressing into his scalp. "Gia, don't, please."

He shakes her shoulder, but she's limp and unresponsive.

Russ stands and paces. There's nothing to do with her. She doesn't want an ambulance.

The message remains on the screen. The Lord took Will? So, the Lord just plucked Will's life from his body? Took it to a better place? Bullshit. That's nothing but fairytales. The truth: Will is no place, nowhere, just dead. Gone.

As Russ continues pacing in front of the TV, his balance seems off, as if the room is tilted. His head throbs, and his stomach hurts. He kneels at the foot of the bed, laying his forehead on the mattress, waiting for the room to level out. Uncontrollably, he starts sobbing, tears and snot dripping on the carpet.

The last time he prayed was in Texas. Admittedly, it worked, kind of. He prayed for the end of Glenn the Great.

Two days later, Glenn was arrested. And he's still in prison today.

Now, Russ prays with more intensity than ever before. He prays for a hoax, prays that a hacker wrote that message. He demands it, begs it, daring God to prove he cares.

Russ wipes his nose with his arm and reassembles the remote. Navigating to the social media pages of some of Will's aunts and cousins, Russ knows the prayer has failed. Everyone's posts confirm Will's death; they write about Will being too young to die, being such a beautiful person, being the life of the party, and of course, about their twisted conclusion that God took him to a better place.

Russ pulls his hair until the pain is too much. His face is heated, his neck strained. He springs onto the mattress, mounting and attacking a pillow, striking it for two full minutes.

He lies face down, his head buried into the beaten pillow, muffling his screams.

When Russ finally goes quiet, the tick-tock of the clock comes into focus. Oddly, it soothes Russ, the rhythm of it, the predictability. He shifts his head to a dry spot on the pillow, but his eyes are still leaking, making it newly wet. Through Russ's watery vision, Gia looks blurry. She's slumped, her eyes stuck open, her mouth gaping, saliva pooling in the corner.

Will would be pissed if he saw Gia like that, no one helping her. Russ swings his legs off the mattress. He examines how best to place his arms to lift her onto the bed.

As he squats beside Gia, a vehicle pulls into the driveway. The brakes squeak, and the engine idles. Maybe Tara heard about Will and came back. Russ hurries to the window and peers out the side of the curtain. It's not a Tesla. Of course not—electric vehicles don't idle, combustion engines do, like this truck, a familiar black one. The driver is wearing a cowboy hat. Russ's stomach turns to knots.

The truck door flies open, and Logan steps out.

Russ slides behind the wall, holding the curtain steady, still able to see out the window.

Logan strolls toward the front door, his boots clopping on the asphalt. He studies the house, probably looking for cameras.

Russ's heart thumps.

As Logan climbs the four stone steps to the front door, he smooths his flannel shirt.

On the TV in the guest room, a security app pops up, a notification that someone is at the front door. Russ clicks yes to view, and Logan appears on the screen. He's standing at parade rest, his hands behind the small of his back. His chest—though narrow—is puffed and hardened, his torso tapered, and a big brass belt buckle, engraved with a bear's head, shines at the front of his waist.

Next to Russ, Gia makes a gurgling sound.

Logan presses the doorbell.

The ring comes through the TV speakers, the clang so loud it's earsplitting. Russ fumbles with the remote, frantically trying to turn down the volume. On the screen, Logan looks toward the guest room.

"Hello?" Logan says, readying his finger for another ring.

A man answers. "How can I help you?"

Russ recognizes the voice: Tara's dad is talking remotely.

"Mr. Saay," Logan says, "I'm Tara's friend—we met once, but it's been a while."

"Tara's not here."

"Right. I was just with her a bit ago. She's probably on the plane to LA now. I swung by because I have our friend's phone. It's Russ Burton's. I thought he might be here."

Russ squirms as if bugs are crawling on him.

"Sorry," says Mr. Saay, "since Tara's not there, there would be no reason for any of her friends to be."

Mr. Saay must know Russ and Gia are inside. Not only would he have seen them arrive on camera last night, but Tara would have told him about it, and she would have asked him to keep it quiet, not wanting Logan to find out she helped Gia.

"Right, sorry to bother you," Logan says. "Since I'm here, though, do you mind if I go down to the water and say a prayer for Will? I just keep thinking about him dancing on the beach around the bonfire a while back."

Mr. Saay pauses. "Okay, sure," he says. "Go around back and say your prayer."

Immediately, Russ bolts out of the guestroom, running on his tiptoes down the hall to the sliding glass door, to close and lock it. Russ sees the fruit bowl and the half-eaten strawberries on the patio table. He opens the screen slider and tiptoes to the table, grabbing the bowl, then throwing in the napkin and the strawberry rinds, and finally snatching the juice glass.

From around the corner, footsteps are coming.

Russ hurries inside, easing the door shut while managing to hold on to the juice glass with the same hand. As he flips the lock, a shadow extends to the porch. He slides over, sinking to the kitchen tile, his back against the cherrywood cabinets.

From the glass door, a shadow enters the kitchen. Russ can see the tip of Logan's boot. But with the way Russ is positioned, Logan shouldn't be able to see him.

"Hey, Russ," Logan says, his voice muffled behind the glass. "Come on and open up—it's Logan." He pulls at the door handle. "I have your phone, man."

Russ stays still, holding his breath, the bowl of fruit on his lap.

"Look, I know Gia is here. It's okay. And I know you both are torn up about Will. I heard the news on the way over."

Still holding his breath, Russ feels his ears start ringing. He stays quiet.

"Answer the door, Russ. Why do you keep hiding?"

Silence lingers for a few seconds. Then Logan knocks three times on the glass, quick and aggressive. Russ gasps, then resumes holding his breath.

The shadow moves to the kitchen window, rising and lowering, Logan trying to look through the tiny openings in the slats.

Suddenly, a loud groan comes from the guestroom.

The shadow holds still. Listening.

14

Like a rodent, Russ creeps along the face of the cherry-wood cabinets. He low-crawls on his belly, his heartbeat drumming against the cold tile. At the corner, he stretches his neck forward, elongating the ligaments, maxing the elasticity, to peek onto the deck. The boots are gone. But Logan is probably hiding, waiting for Russ to come out, waiting to strike.

From down the hall, from the guest bedroom, Gia groans like a wounded animal. Russ flinches, then freezes, listening for movement.

After a few minutes, he inches out, the three buttons on his polo shirt scraping the tile. Most of the deck is in view. There's no movement, no shadows.

Gia groans again. Then she screams.

It cuts off quickly, her voice box seeming to turn off prematurely. Russ jumps to his feet and runs for it, dashing on his tiptoes out of the kitchen, down the hall, keeping a bowlegged gate to minimize the swishing of his golf shorts. He slips through the doorway. Gia is on the floor, tipped over, having fallen sideways along the front of the dresser, her head drooped over her shoulder, her face flat on the carpet, the carpet perhaps muffling her scream. Russ scans the room: no predator.

Drool-soaked strands of black hair are pasted to her cheek. Russ kneels next to her and slides his finger across her temple, pulling the strands off her skin. Strings of saliva break away as he tucks the soggy strands behind her ear.

Russ crawls to the window, avoiding the possibility of his shadow appearing on the curtain. As a child, Russ was good at sneaking around, doing his best to stay unnoticed by both his mother and her men. At the wall next to the curtain, Russ gets into a squat and rises like a rodent popping out of his dirt hole. Keeping his back flat against the wall, he peeks through the gap in the curtain.

Logan paces in front of his truck, looking at his cell. For someone who just found out his friend is dead, a friend he rescued from drowning the night before, Logan looks unfazed, almost bored, maybe impatient. Not upset, and definitely not devastated. Logan leans against the grill of his truck. He looks up from his phone and peers at the guestroom window, his eyes like a hunter's, intense, sensing prey.

Russ freezes.

Gia groans in agony, rolling onto her back, wrapping her arms around her ribcage, seeming to hug herself. She moans, rocking like a baby stuck on its back.

Logan leans off his truck, holding his stare. He steps toward the window, stopping a mere fifteen feet away, raising his arms out wide. "Come on!"

On the TV, the home security app activates, the loading circle spinning, spinning, spinning. Finally, Logan appears, his profile, his hat brim frayed, his jaw clenched. He turns to the light doorbell camera. His eyes narrow, his stare beaming through the camera lens to the screen on the other side. In this case, onto the TV in the guest bedroom.

Russ presses harder against the wall as if attempting to sink into it. Gia grunts, trying to push herself up, a string of saliva dangling from her mouth. Russ puts his finger to his lips, tapping, tapping, but she's not looking, she's not coherent. Gia collapses back onto her stomach. From outside, Logan shouts, "I know you're in there!"

His voice propels through the TV speakers, piercing Russ's nervous system like needles blasted from a shotgun. Russ jolts, his shoulder bumping the curtain, sending a wave through the fabric like the flap of a giant flag.

Mr. Saay's voice shoots through the speakers. "Excuse me?"

Logan hustles onto the porch and stands in front of the camera like a boy beckoned by his father. "Hi, sir," he says, wagging the phone at the camera, "I'm trying to send my texts before I get to driving, but it's giving me trouble."

"You said you know I'm in there."

Logan laughs nervously. "No, sir, not you—the stupid voice-control in my phone. I know she's in there, Siri, but she never works."

Mr. Saay clears his throat. "Look, Logan, I keep getting notifications from my security camera, and I'm in meetings today."

"Right, sorry," Logan says, taking a step back. "Thank you again. I'll be getting out of here."

Inside the guestroom, the curtain is still, as is Russ against the wall, as is Gia unconscious on the floor.

On the TV screen, Logan turns to leave.

When the truck is gone, having taken a left out of the driveway, Russ comes off the wall, the back of his shirt soaked with sweat. He's soon pacing again, pulling back his hair.

Gia groans.

Russ straddles her and slips his arms under her shoulders, hooking her, lifting. Her head flops back onto his chest. As he pulls her body, her legs drag on the carpet. He positions her in between the columns of dresser knobs and props her against the furniture.

Then he takes a breath, rubs his temple, and goes back to pacing.

The security app is gone from the TV, and the home screen awaits a command. He should send a message to the police, an online complaint, tell them everything: that Logan probably shocked Will—in front of an entire party—and then "saved" him to cover it up. And then probably came after Gia, pretending to be there to return Russ's cell phone. Russ shakes his head. Maybe adding the bit about the dead crow on Will's truck would help. Sure, a dead animal on a big truck—big deal.

Why a crow? Why would Logan pick that particular animal? Maybe Logan found it dead. There are a ton of crows around here, so they're easy to find. Maybe he found it already hit by a vehicle. If Logan had put a lamb or something like that on Will's truck, the intent would have been obvious. But, still, why a crow? They eat anything, they are everywhere, cities and forests and farms. Yes, farms. Crows are the enemy of farmers, taking what the farmers see as rightfully theirs. And, of course, Logan is a farmer. So, it's what, a dead enemy on another enemy's hood? Or maybe the crow just crashed into the windshield and died on the truck.

Either way, now, Will is dead just like the crow. Gia is next, obviously. Probably. There's no way Logan would seek out Russ to deliver his cell phone. Come on. Gia is in trouble, in more ways than one, and Russ is mixed up in it.

The room seems to tip again. He braces himself on the bed. His body flashes hot, and he hurries for the toilet. Stumbling into the bathroom, he grabs the porcelain bowl and heaves. The chunks plop into the water, and the water and bits of it spray back at Russ's face.

Not wanting to drip onto the floor, he keeps his face over the toilet as he reaches blindly for the flush handle, sending the puke down the hole, the water swirling. A gush of air smacks his face. He's still dizzy, but the room starts to level.

He washes his face and brushes his teeth with his finger—for the second time today.

His stomach is weak and his limbs are limp as he shuffles out of the bathroom. Gia is on the floor again, but she's trying to get up. She's on her hands and knees, rocking, her hair draped over the front of her head, her split ends grazing the carpet.

"Will's gone," she whispers. "Isn't he?"

Russ hasn't admitted it out loud. He read the message, of course, but he hasn't verbally confirmed it to another human. Doing so will somehow make it final. He puts his hand on her shoulder blade. The words start to come up, but he chokes them down.

"Tell me, please," she says, softly. "Tell me I was dreaming." She rocks back and forth like a child distracting herself from pain.

Russ lets out the words: "The Lord took him to a better place." He hangs his head, stunned that he barfed up that phrase.

Gia crumples to the floor, sobbing, telling Russ no over and over.

He sits against the dresser, his face in his hands, the wooden knobs digging into his back. Death would be a relief. Why bother with all this? Why not go to a better fucking place? What a monster, letting people fry in pools, or having them shamed publicly, or leaving them alone with no one to love them. A fucking monster.

The ticking of the clock comes into focus. Russ stands. He hasn't cried like this before, not with someone else in the room.

He wipes his eyes. "We got to get out of here," he says, standing up.

Gia's forehead is flat on the carpet. "Logan did this," she says, leaving her lips parted like she's a beached fish.

Through the gap in the curtain, Russ checks the front. "He's probably waiting for us to leave."

Summoning every bit of her energy, Gia wills herself to her feet, grunting, then yelling, "I hope he hurries up and gets it over with!" She stumbles like a drunkard to the curtain.

Russ tries to intercept her, but he's thrown off guard, surprised, and she flings open the curtain. "I'm right here. I'm right fucking here."

"No," Russ pleads, wrestling the curtain closed.

He holds Gia, letting her punch his back, letting her sobs ring in his ears. Although Russ is no longer crying, although he can, even in this momentous moment, tuck away his pain, they share this hurt, this fear. They hold each other as the time ticks away.

"I think we should let the police know," Russ says.

She sits on the bed. "What can you really tell them?"

"They should at least check out Logan."

"It's an easy closed case for them. And besides that, if I show up, they'll probably detain me—a convict—for some bullshit reason. I'm on parole. I'll probably die in custody while this disease takes me out . . . but maybe that wouldn't be so bad."

Russ grabs the remote. "I can probably file something online, anonymously."

"Suit yourself," she says, standing, finding her balance before lumbering to the door. "I'll get some supplies."

Confused, Russ looks up from the TV.

"You'll still give me a ride, right?" she asks.

"Well, yeah, of course, but we'll probably need to wait . . ." He points to the curtain. "Logan is—"

"I don't have the luxury of waiting. You see me, passing out, drooling on myself."

Russ nods.

Gia smiles, scrunching the red, irritated skin around her bloodshot eyes. She leaves the room.

Next to the doorway is Tara's note, crinkled and leaning on the wall. Take care of Gia, Tara had written. She is counting on Russ.

And he owes it to Will.

Russ navigates to the Seattle Police Department's website and finds the tip submission page in seconds. He keeps it simple, to the point:

Logan Price probably killed Will Bayman.

Killed? It's so surreal—Will was probably murdered. The room starts to go off kilter. Russ hurries and clicks submit, trying to get the word off the screen.

He breathes deeply, closing his eyes, searching for a happy place in his mind. He sees himself in LA.

Once he settles, he finds Tara's page. The first photo: Will and Tara, laying her head on his shoulder, a picture from last summer at the Coop. Before his eyes can well up from seeing Will's face, he scrolls down, looking for more pictures. There's one: a picture of Tara on the beautiful UCLA campus, her arms wide as if she's ready to fly. As he tries to imagine himself as the one who had taken the picture, he can't help but ruminate on the photo from the

Coop. It's possible Will and Tara hooked up that night. Russ focuses harder on the UCLA photo.

Gia barges in, a pink backpack over her shoulder, a key fob dangling from her finger.

Russ fumbles the remote as if he's been busted looking at something naughty.

"You got it bad, don't you," Gia says.

"What?" Russ picks up the remote.

"I got you a disguise." She holds up a gray fedora in one hand and reading glasses in another. "You'll be Tara's grandpa as we drive out of here."

She tosses him the key fob.

15

In the garage is a Jeep Wrangler. Wrangler reminds Russ of Logan's jeans and the chew can imprint on Logan's butt. And butt reminds him of his new nickname.

Russ shakes his head, trying to provoke a new string of thoughts, as if his brain is a magic eight-ball, like the one Jeremiah the Bullfrog kept on the coffee table, the eight-ball Russ once used to ask if Tara loved him back—outlook not so good.

The tires are oversized and knobby. Gia opens the rear passenger side door. Her steadiness is much improved. She steps onto the running board and crawls into the back seat. Lying down, she uses the backpack as a pillow.

Russ shuts the door behind her, careful not to bang her feet. The door latches like a sealed hatchway designed with precise engineering, the click satisfying. He's dreamed of driving Tara on a date in a vehicle like this, but he hasn't found anything affordable yet. Although he got his license expecting to secure a new ride in short order, it's been two years with no progress.

So now, to make matters worse, he has very little driving experience.

Russ walks around the front of the Jeep, between the grill and the garage door, the only barrier between them and Logan. He takes a deep breath before getting in the driver's seat. The seats are black leather with red, weblike stripes. The headrests have stitched-in spiders, black widows, some special-edition décor.

Russ clicks in his seat belt and examines the controls as if he's a pilot executing a preflight check list: he caresses the gear selector, pumps the brake, checks the dashboard. Above him, clipped to the visor, is the garage door opener, the no-going-back button. Once the door is raised, they'll be exposed.

He puts on the fedora and glasses and checks himself in the rearview. He looks more like a drama nerd than an old guy. Peering over the top of the glasses, the lenses too thick, too blurry for direct use, he turns back to Gia.

"Do you think we should get ahold of Tara just to make sure we can take the Jeep?" Russ asks.

"She already said it was okay."

Russ sets his hands on the steering wheel at the ten and two positions. He stares at the garage door, envisioning the other side and how driving out might go down. Perhaps Logan isn't waiting, and they'll glide freely on their way. If he is waiting, perhaps he mistakes

Russ for an old man, and they sneak past. But if Logan knows it's them . . . then what?

Russ engages the no-going-back button. The garage door begins lifting, its motor buzzing. Sunlight enters, expanding onto the front tires, onto the winch, onto the windshield. Russ engages the Jeep's ignition.

When there's just enough clearance, before the door is fully up, Russ begins inching forward. As the Jeep rolls onto the driveway, in view of the doorbell camera, Russ wonders if Mr. Saay will notice him borrowing his fedora and glasses, not to mention his vehicle.

Halfway down the driveway, Gia says, "Hunch over."

Russ swallows hard and arches his back, putting his line of sight over the top of the steering wheel. His palms sweat. He drives slow, extra slow, old-man slow. The driveway is so long. Russ envisions Logan's truck flying around the corner, barreling up the driveway, playing chicken. Logan's favorite. How fitting would that be—playing chicken in the pool, playing chicken up the driveway.

As Russ approaches the street, his head huddled between his shoulders, he looks left, then right. No sign of Logan's truck. In fact, there are no trucks at all, just an assortment of sedan-style EVs and sports cars awaiting their sleepy owners on a Sunday morning. With the same hope as someone playing Russian roulette, Russ taps the gas and turns onto the street. Keeping his hunched posture, he increases the pace incrementally, checking the rearview over and over. He doesn't want to celebrate too early, but so far, so good.

"So, which way am I going?" Russ asks, straightening up.

"Are we good?" Gia asks.

Russ double checks his rearview. "I don't see anything."

Gia remains lying down. "Just start going. There's a GPS on the dash we can use once we get away from here. It's like a three-hour drive, so we have plenty of time."

Three hours away—a welcome distance from Logan. And once they find Gia's dad, Russ can call Tara and let her know. Hell, maybe he'll tell her in person. What's more, Logan won't know for sure if Russ was inside the lake house, nor if he helped Gia.

As Russ comes to a stop sign, he pushes up the glasses, which are slipping down his nose.

"How are you feeling?" Russ asks.

"I'm just tired—"

"Oh shit!"

In his rearview, a black truck appears. Logan's truck. Russ hunches back over and accelerates through the intersection, jerking the Jeep.

"Is it him?" Gia says.

Russ doesn't answer as he slows the Jeep to old-man speed.

Logan follows them through the intersection, nosing the truck's grill close to the Jeep's spare tire, mounted to its rear. Logan is probably trying to see in, but the rear windows are tinted limo-black. The tint on the fronts, however, is lighter, and the windshield has a thin strip of tint along the top.

Logan creeps even closer, his left tires drifting over the center line. Russ speeds up. Logan accelerates.

When Russ taps the brakes, Logan slingshots around the rear of the Jeep into wrong-way traffic, the truck's engine roaring as its front end gains on the Jeep's.

Russ hunches more. He taps his horn with his right hand and shakes his fist at Logan, leaving the left arm to block his face.

Logan cuts in front, forcing Russ onto the shoulder. Russ slams the brakes as Logan stops, dust flying up between them.

"Oh my God!" Gia screams.

Logan's door flies open, and he faces the Jeep, marching at it, pointing at Russ.

Russ freezes.

Through the dust, Logan approaches.

"Do something," Gia pleads.

Russ shakes his fist again, keeping the old geezer shtick going.

Logan keeps coming, his jaw clenched, his head tilted down, locked on to Russ under the brim of his cowboy hat.

Gia pops up in her seat. "Go!" she orders.

Russ punches the gas, turning a hard left, rocks spitting out the tires. Logan raises his arm as if he's about to smash the passenger side window.

Russ blows past Logan, swerving the Jeep onto the road.

He checks the rearview. Logan is hopping on one foot.

"Oh shit, oh shit," Russ says.

Gia keeps looking out the back, shouting, "Go, go, go!"

16

Although Russ is no longer acting like an old geezer, he hunches over the steering wheel, his focus on the street. He speeds through the neighborhood, but the Jeep is not getting the distance they need. It's as if the asphalt is a treadmill belt slipping under the tires. The speedometer climbs to eighty. In his periphery, white lines and parked cars streak past. To his front, there's a slow Sunday-morning driver, their brake lights bright, despite the green traffic signal ahead. Russ flies around them, through the intersection, the engine screaming, the knobby tires vibrating.

People who are being chased typically look back, slowing down, unintentionally and unnecessarily. Russ doesn't even glance at the rearview, keeping his focus ahead, mostly to maintain maximum speed while maintaining maximum concentration, but also because part of him doesn't even want to know if Logan is back there, if he hobbled back to his truck and punched the gas. Russ drives like he's playing a video game, a racing game, the controller's go-button pinched down.

He weaves around another vehicle. The driver, an actual old man, blares his horn and flips him off.

Gia sits up, scrambling for her seatbelt. She clicks it in and looks back. "Slow down, we're fine."

Russ keeps the gas pedal pressed. He doesn't know exactly where to go, but his only freeway option now is WA-16 toward Tacoma. He swerves for the onramp.

"Slow down," Gia pleads. "You're going to get us pulled over."

Being pulled over doesn't sound too bad. At least they'd be shielded from Logan, temporarily. Nonetheless, Russ slows the Jeep to match the flow of freeway traffic, and he finally checks his rearview.

Expecting to see Logan, Russ tenses, but the truck isn't there, just random vehicles—and Gia in the corner of the mirror staring at him, smirking, as if they just got away with a crime. Really, they haven't gotten away with anything. They're fleeing, still exposed. What's for sure, however, is that Russ has in fact committed a crime: a hit-and-run. He ran over Logan's foot and kept going. It was self-defense, of course, but proving that would be another matter. Logan didn't have a weapon or make any threats. Although Logan's face—mean like the devil—made his intentions clear, a facial expression wouldn't prove anything.

There's a bridge ahead. Vehicles begin to stop, their brake lights like little red bricks blocking its entrance. If Logan is pursuing them, this is where he'll catch up.

As the Jeep's knobby tires come to a stop, the engine fan buzzes, and the scent of overheated metal and belts wafts through the vents.

"You smell that?" Gia asks.

Russ's finger hovers in front of the a/c controls. "I wasn't even going that fast," he says, pressing the air recirculation button, closing off outside airflow to the cab.

"Seemed fast to me," she says, rubbing her chest.

"Maybe for a residential area, but the Jeep should be fine." Russ checks the dashboard: the red needle on the temperature gauge is within the acceptable range. He checks the rearview. Cars pack behind the Jeep, creating a buffer between them and Logan, should he be coming.

"He won't be back there," Gia says. "He needs an ambulance."

"You really think so?"

"I really hope so."

The Jeep enters the bridge. As they creep forward, they ascend like it's a roller coaster.

Russ's grip tightens on the steering wheel. If Logan goes to the hospital, he'll have to explain how his foot was injured.

"I wasn't trying to hit him," Russ says, "I—"

"Well, he was trying to kill us."

A coldness hits Russ's core, and his skin tingles like he's being pricked with a pin all over. Kill. Murder.

"How can you be sure?"

"He shocked Will to death. You know it, and I know it. Then he shows up at Tara's lake house, what, to return your phone? Yeah, right. Then he runs us off the road and charges at us like some evil animal. You saw his face, his eyes. You know."

The Jeep approaches the top of the bridge.

"We're calling the cops," Russ says.

"We still have nothing to tell them." Gia gazes at the water, a narrow section of the Puget. "And if we get the police involved, Logan will press charges—to get the heat off him and onto you."

"He'll do that anyway. We need to beat him to it. I could go to jail for this." Russ pulls back his hair and glances in the rearview at Gia, someone who's been in prison, someone who probably doesn't want to hear the whining about maybe getting arrested.

"Logan doesn't want the cops involved, and neither do we," Gia says, lowering her window. "So, don't you worry, you're not going to jail. Now, if he ends up in cuffs, I'm telling you, that could be a different story. He may as well take you down."

The Jeep crests, picking up momentum on the down-side as traffic loosens. Sickness rises in Russ's stomach, but he orders it away. Somehow, that works.

Gia sets her hand on his shoulder. "All we have to do is get off this bridge and find I-5. You did good." She leans back. "Will is proud of you. I can feel it."

She sets the backpack on her lap and pulls out a pair of scissors. Lifting her leg, she snips her ankle monitor, then holds the rubber strap in front of her like a stinky dead animal. After a few seconds, she flings it out the window and over the side of the bridge.

17

Accelerating, the Jeep enters the I-5 North onramp, the engine roaring, the tires rumbling over grooves in the pavement, the chassis vibrating like a jetliner taking off.

Now, cruising on a new freeway, in a new direction, without the cowboy's truck in the rearview, it's safe to say Logan isn't following. However, that could mean he's hurt badly, unable to chase. A severe injury would make a potential defense against a hit-and-run charge more difficult. But Russ can't think about that now. They need more distance between the Jeep and Seattle. While holding the wheel with his left hand, Russ holds his abdomen with his right.

Gia climbs up front, her leg brushing Russ's shoulder, her touch momentarily calming him. She smiles at the open road, her cheeks high on her face, seemingly stuck there. She doesn't verbalize her obvious elation, perhaps not believing it appropriate—or perhaps she worries gloating could jinx their good fortune. Instead, she sits quietly, marinating in the spoils of their escape, the speaker cutting out. After a moment's pause, Russ laughs too. He hangs his head and laughs even harder. Gia steadies herself on a bench-sized piece of driftwood next to the backpack and sits down. She wipes her eyes and lets her laughter calm until it comes intermittently, like the waves lapping ashore.

Russ sits next to her. "Whoops, not exactly like Will," he says.

"You have sand on your knuckles," Gia says, brushing it off his fingers.

She leans back and closes her eyes, letting the setting sun have her neck. Gia's time in prison has changed her appearance, making her look pale and frail, but she's still exceptional. Russ studies the sunlight warming her skin. She lifts her eyelids slightly and catches him looking. She chuckles, and he snaps his stare to the ground.

"It's nice," she says, closing her eyes again.

"The sun?" Russ asks, grabbing a stick and doodling in the moist sand.

"That too. But I mean getting checked out by a normal guy—instead of fat and married prison guards."

"Oh, I wasn't—"

"I'm hungry," she says, leaning forward and grabbing the backpack, which she sets on her knees. "Protein bar or trail mix?"

"Uh, bar," Russ says, still drawing. "Please."

They chew granola bars laced with chocolate, the sweetness intense after a day with little food. They stare at the beauty in front of them. It's fascinating how something so beautiful can be so dangerous, the perilous wild. But in this moment, they're safe, and that in and of itself is comforting.

Then again, it's only partially satisfying. Will isn't here, so how could they feel any real joy right now? Nonetheless, Russ does, and he's certain Gia does too.

"Do you feel that?" she asks.

"What?"

"I can feel him."

Russ shifts on the log. "Who . . ."

She stands up. Like a wolf, she howls across the lake, her hands cupped around her mouth, pieces of granola flying out.

Russ stands, looking up and down the beach, trying to figure out what's going on.

She howls again.

Russ begins breathing heavily.

Gia stops and turns suddenly, snatching the backpack, shoving her hand inside. She pulls out a bottle of Jägermeister she must have grabbed from the lake house's liquor cabinet. "I feel him." Holding it with two hands, she kisses the bottle.

Chills roll up Russ's neck.

off his boot. Next, he peels off his sock, revealing his three black-and-blue toes and a swollen foot. He decides nothing is broken.

Logan cracks the whiskey cap and throws it into the darkness. He thinks about pouring some out for his father, but he decides not to share. His father loved this place. He'd come when going for sobriety, usually after being sober for a short period, a period that extended beyond four days of withdrawal and sickness. Although sobriety never lasted long—two months at best—Logan enjoyed those rare occasions. They would hike the trails here, between the mess of spindly branches on skinny trees jetting out of the earth in wild directions. Many of them had no leaves, dying beneath the large trunks of the towering sun hogs. They would stop at a clearing between two beastly pines, spaced like uprights on a goal post, creating a natural window to the Puget Sound. His father dubbed it Logan's Landing. Those hikes were the only time his father would give him advice, instead of farming instruction. He would say things like, "The berry is not made for your benefit, it's made for the bush's."

Logan takes a pull off the bottle. He would bring Keely here sometimes. They'd laugh loudly, just them, separated from the entire world. There was no social pressure, no other people. They would make plans to start their own farm, somewhere in a different state, maybe Montana. Keely wanted to be an elementary school teacher.

That surprised Logan, because she was a little shy and hated talking in front of a crowd. She was also absolutely gorgeous, even though she didn't think so, stemming mostly from kids in middle school poking fun at her nerdy look, glasses over freckles.

Although Logan found Keely's insecurities somewhat cute, there was a major downside. When Keely got attention from other guys, she lapped it up. This drove Logan crazy. Logan once seriously injured a guy for hitting on her. That put an end to anyone even subtly flirting with Keely, except for one person: Will Bayman. Will wasn't afraid of Logan, or at least he never showed it. Although Logan didn't enjoy being feared, it bothered him that Will wasn't afraid.

Logan was somewhat understanding of Keely's need for attention, and he never believed she would be unfaithful. She loved him. So, when rumors started going around about Keely hooking up with Will, Logan went on the offensive, getting in Will's face. Bayman denied it. Of course, Keely denied it too. Logan was skeptical, however, because he had seen them flirting. Ultimately, he believed Keely, but not Will, as crazy as that sounds. Regardless, when it came to Will's culpability, he was guilty. At the very least, he had flirted with Keely. He was responsible for bolstering the potential legitimacy of the rumors. If Will had just respected what was Logan's, none of this would have ever happened.

When Keely was in the hospital, Logan barely got to see her. Keely's parents weren't that fond of him. He would wait for hours in the waiting room. They would tell him he should go get some rest, but he would decline and stay. It made it harder for them, him being there, but he couldn't stomach the thought of Keely waking up without him.

She lay with an infection for a week before she died. It rocked the high school and the community, even gaining national attention, particularly when Gia became known as the Porta-Potty Pusher. She had already been arrested for assault, but days later, she was charged with manslaughter.

When Keely died, Logan was distraught, oscillating between rage and depression. Part of him wanted to join Keely. The other part of him wanted to avenge her death. He decided he'd do both. First, he would kill Will and Gia. Then, he would join his true love. This would require some patience on his part, and he would have to be smart about it. He would have to play nice with Will for a while, for a long while, until Gia finished her seven-year sentence. If he killed Will before Gia's release, and if he got caught, he wouldn't have a chance to get her.

Her early release was a surprise. At first, Logan was enraged that they let her out. Then, he saw it as an opportunity. He initiated his plan. It was important that Will knew who was responsible for ending him. That was the purpose of the dead crow. The pool accident was perfect, and phase one was complete.

But now, it seems phase two of his plan has failed. Gia is probably headed out of the country, probably gone for good. Logan grabs his phone.

"Northwest Suicide and Crisis Lifeline, this is Treena. Who am I speaking with today?"

"Calling for Chad, please."

"Oh, sir, I'm not certain if Chad is working, but I'm available and happy to assist you. Tell me what's happening at the moment."

"Treena, get Chad, okay?"

"Um . . . Let me see if he's available, one moment."

The line goes silent. Logan examines the pistol. The revolver became his after his father's death, but he already knew the gun well. He'd go target shooting with it in the backwoods, using pinecones as targets.

"This is Chad," a voice says.

"Chad, it's Larry Washington," Logan says.

"Mr. Washington, I'm glad you called, but I cannot be your personal chat counselor—everyone here is qualified and can assist you."

"I'm not going to reexplain everything to someone else, Chad."

"I understand." Chad clears his throat. "Mr. Washington, are you in a safe place?"

Logan looks around the darkness. He's totally alone, in the woods. The only sounds are the crickets and the occasional bug buzzing by his ear. "Seems safe enough, but you never know what's lurking, I guess."

"You alone?"

"No, not really. I got you, Chad."

"Yes, Mr. Washington, but it would be good if you had people around you."

"Why do you do this job, Chad?"

"Well, if I can help, I want to do that."

"What if you make things worse? How would you deal with that."

"That's definitely something I don't want. If I can't be helpful to others, I'll find something else."

"But it's too late after that. Let me ask you—you ever had someone, you know, do it on the phone?"

"Mr. Washington, I can't talk about other clients, and that's really not an appropriate question. Are you having thoughts about harming yourself?"

"Harming?" Logan scoffs. "Like blasting one right through the ole blood pumper?" He aims the gun at the night's sky, at a satellite drifting along.

"Do you have a firearm, Mr. Washington?"

Logan straightens up. "Does it really matter, Chad? I could jump off a cliff if I didn't have one."

"It does matter. And if you do have one, can you leave it where you are, in a safe place, and go somewhere else, maybe a coffee shop, or visit with a supportive family member?"

"The only way I'm seeing family is on the other side of a bullet."

"What do you mean?"

"There's no one left to visit."

"I'm sorry. Is there a friend you could call?"

Logan doesn't answer.

"Well, I'm here with you, Mr. Washington. We can talk about anything you want."

Logan takes a drink of whiskey. "Great. Be honest. Do you think it's wrong for someone to end it?"

"If you're asking me if it's okay for someone to take their own life, that's never okay."

"I've got to be honest. I think that is a little *dishon-est*. What if someone endures severe, endless suffering? What about then?"

"We sometimes envision the future with the same sadness or pain we have in the present—"

"Get off the cheat sheet, Chad."

"I have no cheat sheet. You accused me of that last time, Mr. Washington, and I don't appreciate that, sir. I'm being as honest and straightforward as I know how."

"Well, let me ask you this. Do you think those who take their own lives go to hell?"

"You should talk to a priest if you have religious questions."

In the dirt below the tailgate, a beetle is flipped on its back, its many legs wiggling.

"One more question, Chad. Why do people write notes?"

"What do you mean?"

"You know what I mean. A suicide note."

"Mostly to explain why they did it. But also, to leave something behind."

"I don't have time to chit-chat anymore, Chad. I've got some writing to do."

"Mr. Washington—"

"Best to you Chad, and by the way, you look good without that goatee."

The call ends.

Logan takes a small notepad from his shirt pocket. His father always wanted him to carry one. It was something he'd learned in the military. On the farm, it came in handy for writing down measurements, listing supply orders, and making reminders.

Logan begins writing. At first, it's cathartic, but as he keeps going, his anger at God begins to fill the page.

He puts the note pad back in his pocket and picks up the pistol from the tailgate and cocks the hammer. As he presses the barrel against his heart, he begins his final prayer, out loud, in the darkness. "Lord, there's nothing left for me in this world. I will leave it having committed the ultimate sin. I have killed once and will do it once more, now. I pray you can find a way to forgive me." His hand is steady, his jaw clenched. "Lord, *please* forgive me. In your name—"

The tailgate vibrates, the orange phone lighting up and buzzing. It's Russ's mom, Morgan. He sets down the gun and stares at the missed call notification. He tries to listen to the message, but the phone is locked.

He studies the lock screen, contemplating what Russ might have used as his code. Logan doesn't know much about Russ—aka Will's shadow. It's probably Will's birthday. Logan chuckles out loud. What else does he know about Russ? He's a valedictorian. His speech sucked, and he got spanked. Crazy. He gave props to his mom during the speech, so maybe it's her birthday. How could Logan figure that out, though? He decides to start simple and tries 1-2-3-4. The phone buzzes—incorrect. One out of ten attempts used. He may as well use nine more before going back to the pistol. He tries 1-1-1-1. Eight left. He tries their graduation year. Seven left.

As he thinks about Russ more deeply, he remembers that Russ has a thing for Tara. He even defended her during his speech. What's Tara's birthday? Logan knows this—she and Keely had birthdays one year and one day apart. Incorrect. Six left. He stares at the numbers, and as he does, he notices the little letters under each. He spells out her name: T (8) - A (2) - R (7) - A (2). Unlocked.

"Are you fucking kidding me?" Logan says, hopping off the tailgate.

He opens Russ's texts. There are a bunch from Morgan. "Damn, Russ. Got yourself kicked out. I would have never guessed."

He checks his notifications next. There are so many about Russ getting spanked. "Ouch."

Logan looks at the apps on the home screen, considering what social media accounts to try, but for some reason he taps on a journaling app next instead. He can't get in; there's a secondary code different from the one that worked on the phone. Then he sees the Find My app. He opens it. Russ's cell phone is at Cougar Mountain Park with Logan, of course, but another device shows up.

Russ's AirTag for AirPods has been located—at Diablo Lake.

19

With a clammy finger, Russ swipes crust from the corner of his eye. His other eye—blurry, but already cleared of gunk—focuses on the road as he drives toward the ferry's parking lot.

Russ woke hot in the middle of the night, the heater still blasting. He killed the engine and drifted back to sleep. He was lucky to have done so, saving some gas in the tank, the gauge now a tick above empty.

It's a quarter until seven, just fifteen minutes before the ferry departs. Russ guides the Jeep into a parking stall, squeezing in between two pickup trucks, both fitted with camper shells. Not yet fully awake, he thrusts the gear selector forward before coming to a complete stop, jolting the Jeep, jarring Gia in the passenger seat and frightening a woman crossing the parking lot to their front. The woman's gray hair is pulled back tight into a ponytail, tugging on the edges of her wrinkled face. She scowls but keeps moving, shaking her head and holding her bloated stomach where it pooches out under her sundress.

The ferry is docked and boarding passengers. It has a silver bottom, a blue top, and six windows on each side. At the end of the dock, a jolly man with a beer belly, his face stubbled white, his head decorated with a captain's hat that's one size too small, waves and points at the handful of people buzzing about. He greets passengers with a thunderous laugh as they give him tickets or cash before walking down the dock and boarding the boat. All but a few passengers seem old. There's no color in their hair, and their bodies limp along as if each and every one has something broken.

The ferry, gently bobbing in the turquoise water, is poised to haul its passengers across Diablo Lake to the base of Ross Dam. From there, passengers will make their way—either by vehicle or hiking—up to Ross Lake.

As Russ gets out of the Jeep, his AirPods charging case falls from his pocket, smacking the ground, and the earbuds shoot out under the vehicle. He squats next to the front tire. Reaching behind the wheel, he pats the asphalt. Searching, swiping, he comes up empty. With the ferry minutes from departure, Russ lies on his stomach. The AirPods are halfway under the truck. He wiggles underneath the Jeep and collects them, pegging each earbud back into its case.

As he stands, Russ brushes asphalt crumbs off his polo shirt. He puts the case back in his pocket and locks the door to the Jeep. Just a few hours from now, he should be back. He'll get gas and then . . .

And then what? Go back to Seattle? There's nothing there anymore, except Will's dead body. There'll be a service, and Russ needs to be there, but Logan could show up, his foot mangled, waiting to get to Russ alone. Or the cops could be there and arrest Russ for the hit-and-run. His blood goes cold. For just a second, he has an impulse to call Will, but he recognizes quickly that calling his best friend will never again be an option. Maybe he could call Tara though, or he could stay with her in LA. She'd be pleased with him for getting the job done, getting Gia to her dad. She might even know what to do about Logan.

"Where are you, Russ?" Gia asks. "We've got to get on board."

Snapping back to the present, Russ pats his shorts, checking for his phone out of habit. "Shit," he says, "Logan has my cell. I use it to pay for everything."

Gia sets the backpack on the hood. "No worries," she says, unzipping and digging through the main compartment. "I got it." She pulls out a plastic baggie with a thin stack of cash.

Russ smiles in relief. "Is that backpack like a magic hat or something. What else is in there?"

uine, so youthful, contrasting with the old, weathered faces of the seniors all around, their smiles denture-filled or yellow. Even so, they seem just as happy. Ironically, despite the stark differences in age, Gia is likely the one closest to death.

An old man with a rough, stubbly, salt-and-pepper beard pats Russ's shoulder. "You're a lucky man," he says.

Russ turns to him, leaning in close. "Oh, we aren't—"

"She is just wonderful," the man's wife says. "You are very lucky." With wide eyes, she nods directly at Russ, as if to say, *Isn't she?*

"Yes, she is very wonderful," Russ says.

"What do you find most beautiful about her?" the woman asks.

"Well . . ." Russ rubs the back of his neck.

"Be honest—life's too short for shyness."

The old man pipes in. "My favorite thing about Marge is that heinie."

Marge smacks the man on the white hairs springing from the open button on his Hawaiian shirt. "Stop it, Harold." She turns to Gia. "He's got a point, though."

Gia gives her a sly grin. Then she puts her hand on Russ's knee. "Well?"

"Well, what?"

"You know what. Don't be shy." Gia straightens up, wiggles, and grins.

At least three old men dial up their hearing aids.

Russ swallows and tries to fight the redness from appearing on his cheeks. He clears his throat. "That's so easy. It's your smile."

"Aww," several passengers moan.

"You lily-livered . . ." Harold sneers, leaning back onto his seat.

"Ah, yes," Marge says, "he's a keeper."

The shuttle crests the top of the hill. Appearing outside their windows is Ross Lake, the water as turquoise as Diablo, which is no surprise, of course, since one feeds the other. But the turquoise is so striking, it's hard for Russ not to notice. The color seems out of place, as if it's from somewhere tropical, not from the mountains.

As the seniors make their way to a large, pontoon-style water taxi, Gia leads Russ to a six-seat ski boat. The pontoon will be going straight across the lake, a five-minute ride to the row of cabins, service staff, and amenities along the shore. Gia and Russ will have a much longer trip to the area of her dad's cabin.

Sitting in the driver's seat of the ski boat is a shirtless twenty-something, who introduces himself as Cormac. He stands to greet them, gripping Russ's shoulder and shaking his hand while winking at Gia.

Russ sits in the middle row. The breeze carries the scent of pine, and the sun reheats his skin, which was cooled by the A/C in the shuttle van. His overall state is warm. Gia's voice, as she talks with Cormac, is joyous, and the kiss on the ferry replays in the background of Russ's mind.

Cormac is muscular and tan. His retro shades, with neon-green frames, show Gia's reflection in the lenses from the angle Russ is sitting at. Gia says something about the cabin, and Cormac nods, pointing up the long, river-like lake.

Gia takes a seat next to Russ, her legs touching his. Cormac starts the engine and reverses the boat away from the dock. As he shifts into forward gear, easing the boat in the direction of their destination, he looks at Gia in the rearview.

"Wanna drive?" he asks.

"Me?" she asks.

"Yeah, you."

"What, are you trying to get me to sit on your lap?"

"Your boyfriend is right there. I would never do that in front of him." As the boat ambles forward, he stands and presents the captain's chair to her. "It's all yours."

Gia gets up and giggles. She sits behind the wheel and looks over the controls. "You going to teach me?"

Russ squirms in his seat.

"This here is the throttle," Cormac says. "To go forward, push it forward, but easy. Just back it off to slow down. This here is the steering wheel. Keep the boat between the shores."

Gia looks up at Cormac, waiting for permission.

"Go for it."

She eases the lever forward. The motor growls louder, the water swishing along the sides. There are no other people or boats in sight, just the wild. It's as if the lake is all hers.

Russ grips the sides of his seat as the boat slices through the surface like a glass cutter. Gia throttles up a little more. In the rearview, her eyes sparkle like the water, her expression one of freedom.

They go for what seems like at least an hour, deep into the wilderness, passing campgrounds but no campers. Finally, Cormac pats her shoulder and points ahead. Gia backs down the throttle, bringing the wind to a near halt. She gets up, smiling and thanking Cormac, who winks.

"You're a natural," he says, climbing back into the captain's chair. "I'll get you guys into Winnebago Flats. There's a dock over there. You'll have to cross into Canada yourselves, though, to get to the cabin."

Russ's ears are ringing. It hits him that they'll actually be leaving the country. He gets a rolling feeling in his stomach.

Gia stands, looking over the windshield, watching the shoreline get closer, an empty and sandy area with campground markers and picnic benches.

Cormac guides the boat to a weathered wooden dock. He grabs a tie rope. "This is your stop," he says, killing the engine.

Gia climbs out, and Russ follows.

"Will you all need a return ride, or will you be hiking back?" Cormac asks.

Russ can't imagine hiking all that way.

"We'll be here at least one night," Gia says, really meaning that Russ will be there at least one night. She won't be coming back.

"Here's my card," Cormac says, handing it to Russ.

Printed on the plastic card is *C-Dog's Water Taxi and Fun*. Russ wonders how they'll call since they have no phone.

"There's limited cell service," Cormac says, "but you can find pockets. Otherwise, I'm up in this area about once a day." He points to the opposite side of the dock, to a rack holding a long piece of PVC pipe with a plastic orange triangle on one end. "You see that orange flag? You can put that over the pin sticking up on the rack, and I'll pull in when I see it."

Russ examines the flag and the pin.

Cormac starts the boat. "By the way," he says, "this area has gained some attention online. People have been coming here to commit suicide."

Gia covers her mouth.

"It's becoming like the Aokigaharaas Forest in Japan, the suicide forest. It's sad. Rescuers patrol these areas though, trying to find them before it's too late. If you see people in orange shirts with one purple stripe, that's them."

"Thanks for the heads-up," Russ says, swallowing hard.

Cormac reverses off the dock. He gives them a wave and turns the boat down-lake. He throttles up, and in less than thirty seconds he's out of sight.

As the engine tails off, the sounds of nature come into the forefront: a bird flapping to a higher branch, a pinecone falling, the water lapping ashore.

Gia sits on one of five weathered-gray picnic benches.

They remind Russ of the benches at the Coop, which reminds him of Will. He looks around. This is the middle of nowhere, but it's somewhere Russ wants to be at this moment. There's safety and relief in distance.

Gia stares out onto the lake. She closes her eyes and inhales the air like a drug. There's an artlike quality to her beauty, something a Renaissance painter would have been compelled to capture.

When she opens her eyes, she looks at Russ and asks, "Do you believe in heaven?"

Russ folds his arms over his stomach. "I believe in *something*," he says, walking to the bench and sitting next to her. "There's just so much we don't know. That's probably why I like to study the cosmos."

"Sometimes," she says, "when I have an episode, I see the white light people talk about. It's real. It's not just light, though, it's thick, it envelops you, like water or something."

Russ wets his lips. "I've . . . I've seen it."

She angles toward him. "When?"

"In Texas." He picks up a long stick and begins doodling in the sand. "I, uh, was literally almost killed by my mom's boyfriend. This asshole, Glen. I called him Glen the Great."

Gia doesn't press him on the details of what Glen did or the meaning behind the nickname.

"He just despised me, basically for existing. I could never figure out why. One day, he just went off the rails. He said he was tired of my lazy ass, which I didn't understand. I had straight A's, a parttime job, kept my room clean. It didn't matter. He grabbed me from behind and just choked me out. I was in the light, it was thick, like you're talking about. I felt like I was a part of it. And part of me wanted to keep moving into it."

Gia scoots closer and wraps her arms around his upper body. She holds him as he continues.

"I woke up in the hospital, a little disappointed that I woke up at all, if I'm being honest."

His admission combined with her hug makes him want to cry. But he doesn't.

"Glen is still in prison."

Gia doesn't say a word, just keeps holding.

"I'm grateful now, though, that I woke up."

"Me too," she says.

They sit in silence for what seems like minutes.

When she finally let's go, Gia asks, "So, you met Will not long after you got back to Seattle?"

"I knew of him my freshman year, but yeah, I didn't get to know him until I got back, when I started tutoring. That's how we became friends. We got close quick."

"Let me guess, you taught him math, and he taught you how to pick up girls?"

Russ grins. "He definitely helped me come out of my shell. Partway, at least."

She takes the stick from him playfully and begins her own drawing. "Did he ever talk about me?"

"Like I said before, he never told me about anything that happened with y'all. Except for one thing."

She looks up at him.

"He told me he lashed the Fire Ant."

Gia giggles. "That's true. She deserved it, trust me."

They stare at Ross Lake for a while.

"Hey," Russ says, "I was wondering, why didn't Will try to find your dad while you were in?"

"He didn't even know I was sick, not until I told him a couple weeks ago, when I got my initial release papers. I guess I didn't want to scare him away, you know. He was all I had in prison, other than exchanging a few letters with my dad. He really stuck with me. Not that he wasn't seeing other girls. I'm not stupid. But honestly, after the way I acted, after what I did to Keely, it didn't bother me. I was just happy he wanted to stay connected, and of course . . ." She chokes back tears. "I imagined us being together when I got out."

It's Russ's turn to hold her.

"I want you to know something, Russ. I'm very thankful for the way you've treated me," she says, beginning to sob. "Not that I don't deserve it, but people despise me for what I did. Forgiveness is impossible. And nobody wants anything to do with anyone who is unforgivable. And I get it, but they don't understand. Keely was my best friend, and I let my jealousy, my rage—based on some stupid rumor—take over. I never wanted to hurt her the way I did. But I did."

Russ returns the lasting hug, being there, holding her, just letting her cry.

When she settles, Russ lets her go.

"Can I ask one thing about it?" Russ asks.

"Of course," she says, wiping her eyes.

"Who told you that Keely was hooking up with Will?"

"Tara did," Gia says. "She told me she was with a bunch of people at a party, and they could all hear Keely with Will behind a door." She throws the stick in the water. "But it turns out Keely wasn't even at that party, and Tara wasn't with those people. She was in that room with Will."

Russ's eyes grow large. "How did you find out?"

"Will told me."

Russ stands. "You could have confronted her yesterday. You could have—"

"Just like I feel guilty for what I've done, so does she. That's why she showed up yesterday."

21

From Winnebago Flats, Silver Skagit Road runs north to Canada. The road is remote and rarely used, even during the peak camping season. Following the shoreline, the road extends beyond Ross Lake and continues along the Skagit River and deep into the wilderness. Russ and Gia walk along its path. She tells him they have about half an hour until they'll reach her dad's cabin. Although he doesn't own it, he's resided in it for several years. No one has ever made a fuss about his presence. Moreover, no one really knows who owns it—if anyone owns it at all, the structure having been built on public lands decades before.

Pine and cedar trees tower over them. Russ imagines how many suiciders have entered these woods, how many rescuers have been too late, and how many scavengers have feasted. Do people pick this place for beauty, or because they feel a sense of not being alone in their suffering, going to a place where others in despair have chosen the same fate?

"I wonder if your dad has ever saved anyone?" Russ asks, adjusting the backpack straps on his shoulders.

"What?"

"Like one of the suiciders that the water taxi guy was talking about."

"If he has," she says, "he never told me about it."

The gravel crunches under their feet, the cadence of their steps in sync.

"Is there a mailman that comes all this way?" Russ asks.

Gia smiles. "No, I'd have to send my letters to the gift shop at the resort," she says. "He would get water taxi drivers to deliver and check for mail. It could be months before he got my letters. He'd also ask campers to mail things when they got back home. I wonder how many letters were never actually sent." She stops walking abruptly. "Oh look . . ." she points to a brown-and-white sign with the words *International Boundary*. "We're in Canada."

Russ stops too. He's never been out of the country. Now he's with a fugitive, illegally leaving one country and illegally entering another.

"They have those Mounties out here?"

"There's nothing to worry—" She stops and grabs her hamstring. "I don't feel good. My legs . . ." She starts to sit down.

"Wait, wait, here, get on my back." Russ flips the backpack onto his chest and squats in front of her.

As her legs give out, she falls forward onto Russ and wraps her arms around his neck and chest. He hoists her up, locking his arms under her legs. Gia's breathing is heavy in his ear. He steadies his balance and takes the first step forward, then the next.

"You're going to be okay," he says. "We'll be there in no time."

"I can't breathe right."

As he charges up the road, her grip begins to loosen, and Russ's legs are already on fire.

"How do I know where the cabin is?" Russ asks.

"There's a pink ribbon tied around a tree on the left side of the road."

"You got to stay awake for me, Gia—and hold on."

Her body is slipping down. Russ leans forward so that she's flatter on his back. He moves like a soldier carrying a wounded comrade, while keeping his eyes looking ahead for the ribbon.

After forty minutes, Russ can't go farther. He heads to the side of the road, into the tall grass, and sinks slowly to his knees. He lies on his chest and then gently rolls Gia to the side. Her eyes are wide open. What's worse, it doesn't seem like she's breathing. Russ puts his cheek above her mouth. A light gust of air brushes his face.

He stands over Gia, guarding her, looking around the woods for animals, for threats. He has no idea how much farther it is. Maybe they already passed it. An ant crawls across Gia's cheek. Russ swipes it off gently.

He sits her up and hoists her over his shoulder. "Okay," he says, grunting, "let's keep going."

She groans. "It's all water."

"Stay with me. There's plenty of water in the river, and I think I can hear it." Russ continues forward.

His mouth is dry and dusty, but he moves faster now, scanning more trees. Finally, he sees a ribbon, but it's yellow. He continues, searching, and only two minutes later, he finds the pink ribbon.

The trail under the ribbon is partially hidden, but it's obvious enough that someone looking for the trail would know it's there. Russ navigates rocks and twigs, trying to keep Gia steady. As he emerges from the tree line, the river appears, as does the tiny cabin.

Russ climbs up three stairs and sets her on the porch, leaning her back against the railing. He knocks on the door. No answer.

He knocks again. Nothing.

"Hello?" Russ says. "Hello!"

He walks around the back of the cabin. There's one window, and it's boarded. He searches the sandy area at the river's edge, looking for a fishing pole, a gold pan, anything that would indicate someone lives there, but there's nothing.

Gia moans from the porch. Russ hurries to her. She's holding her head and wincing as if she has a migraine. Russ sits on the porch with her.

"You okay?" he asks.

She moans again. "Let me rest for one second," she says in a low voice.

A few minutes pass before she speaks again. "Please tell me my dad is here."

"Nobody's answering," Russ says.

Gia begins to nod off.

Russ goes back around to the rear of the cabin, where he examines the boarded window. There are six nails, four at the corners and two more for good measure. Russ grips the board at the edge and pulls. Impossible.

He searches for something that he can use to pry with. First, he tries to use a flat rock and a round rock—one as a wedge and the other as a hammer. It doesn't work. Next, he tries a rusty can. Not even close. He looks around near the river, at the tree line. Halfway buried in the dirt, he finds what looks like an old grill rack. If he can wedge it between the board and the window frame, he might be able to use it to pry the thing open.

It takes Russ an hour and a half, but finally, the nail in the lower right corner squeaks out of the frame. From there, he works the grill around the board until it pops off. He presses his palm against the window and slides it open. Russ shimmies through. There's nothing inside but an empty table and a bed frame with a worn, full-sized mattress. The cabin is lifeless and smells of dust.

He unlocks the deadbolt and opens the door. Gia is still out of it. He lifts her up and puts her on the bed. Using a sweater from the backpack, he makes her a pillow.

Exhausted, Russ sits on the wood floor, his back propped against the wall. He wants to sleep, but his mind is racing. What will they do next? What if Gia doesn't make it?

His tiredness, mixed with the heat inside the cabin, irritates Russ so much that he gets up, empties his pockets onto the table, and strips down to his boxer briefs, leaving his clothes in a jumbled pile on the floor. He walks out the door and down toward the river, rocks and spiky leaves poking his feet. When he reaches the water, the cool, muddy shore is satisfying on his skin. He walks slowly, carefully, into the flow until he's completely submerged, staying underwater until he's forced to come up for air. As he floats on his back, an oak tree hangs over him like a mother hovering over her child in the bath. Russ does his best not to nod off.

An hour later, in the late afternoon, Gia is coming out of her episode. She tries to sit up, but she can't, so Russ helps. She begins crying on his chest.

"My dad has left for good," she says.

"Yeah, the window was boarded."

"It's over."

"No, don't say that. We'll go back—"

"It's fucking over. I'll never find him in time."

She lies back down on the sweater, on her side, in the fetal position.

"We'll figure something out," Russ says, sitting on the edge of the bed.

"It's over, Russ. How many times do I have to say it? Thank you for everything you've done, but you can go now."

"Don't say that."

She closes her eyes, and tears drip onto the sweater pillow. "Let's be honest," she says," I have no idea where he is—he could be anywhere. He's the only person who might have some answer to this fucking disease, and my time is up. I'm done."

"We'll head back to Seattle and—"

"There's nowhere left for me to go, Russ. Just leave me in peace, please."

"I'm not leaving you here."

"Get out!" she screams. "Now! I don't want you here. Out!"

"Where am I supposed to go?"

"Where are you supposed to go? Listen to yourself. You can go anywhere, do anything. You are young and able. Get out of here, Russ. Go. I'm grateful for how you've helped me. Maybe a part of me knew he wouldn't be here. I'm never going back. This is just the way it is."

She swings her legs off the bed and stands, wobbling. Grabbing his shoulder, she steadies herself and kisses him hard on the lips. It feels like she's not only kissing him goodbye, but everything.

She pushes him toward the door. He doesn't physically resist.

"Wait, wait," he says. "At least let me spend the night."

As he stands on the porch, she grabs the pile of clothes on the floor. "I'm sorry," she says, handing them to him. "Goodbye Russ."

She shuts the door.

Russ stands there for a moment, hoping she'll come to her senses. She doesn't.

He gets dressed and walks up the trail. Under the tree with the pink ribbon, he sits for a while and tries to figure out what to do.

He'll give her some time to cool off, and then he'll head back down to the cabin. If he goes back right now, she might do something rash.

22

By the time Logan gets to Ross Lake, no water taxis are running, and the sun is on its way down. He bypassed Diablo Lake, and the ferry, opting to travel around the east side to the Ross Dam trailhead. Because the parking lot was full, he left his truck on the shoulder, the oversized tires sticking halfway out into the road. He didn't care if it was towed, knowing it would be the last time he would ever drive his truck.

Because there are no water taxis, Logan flags down a couple in a rented ski boat. The driver, a white-haired, white-goateed man with a faded Marines tattoo, studies Logan on the shore. Perhaps it's Logan's cowboy look that intrigues the man, who coasts his boat toward the dock but keeps his distance, cautious.

Logan apologizes and explains that he has no way to get to his friends up by Winnebago Flats, and he was wondering if the man would be kind enough to give him a ride up the lake. The wife seems pleased enough with Logan, his manners and clean look. Using the back of her hand, she pats her husband's bulging gut, a signal to help him out. The man guides the boat to the dock.

They say they can take Logan to Cat Island Campground, where they're staying. If they go any farther, it would be too dark to drive back down safely. Logan is much obliged.

When they arrive, Logan shakes the man's hand using a firm grip, and he exchanges waves with the wife as he heads for East Bank Trail—the way to Russ's AirPods, according to the Find My app. Although the reception is spotty, it's good enough to keep Logan heading in the right direction.

He puts on a headlamp and makes his way up the trail. The moon is covered with clouds, so Logan can only see ten feet of the trail in front of him. He hikes for hours, ten feet at a time, until he finally comes to a yellow ribbon wrapped around a tree. He cuts through the woods, toward the sound of the river, angling toward the location of the AirPods.

A few minutes later, he comes to a cabin. He turns off his headlamp. From the tree line, he crouches, watching for movement. Like a special operator, he hustles for the rear of the structure and takes a position to the side of the window. A piece of plywood is propped below it, and the inside of the cabin is dark. Slowly, he peeks inside. He can't see through the window.

Logan unholsters his revolver and moves around to the front of the cabin, his back against the wood siding. He surveys the area and creeps up the stairs, softly moving up onto the porch. He controls his breathing as he reaches for the handle. The moonlight, although dim, will change the lighting inside the cabin and could wake up the occupants. Ready to shoot, he points his gun at the door and opens it.

Someone is sleeping on the bed. He examines the room for another person, knowing Russ and Gia are together, but he sees no one else. He eases into the room and shuts the door just enough to neutralize the change in light, but not fully closing it so as to avoid waking the sleeper.

He advances toward the bed, his gun aimed at the figure. As he gets closer, he notices something on the floor. Logan stops and clicks on his headlamp. What he sees causes him to lower his gun. He cocks his head to the side and stares at the horrific but satisfying scene in front of him. There's a pool of blood on the floor. Above it is a slashed wrist. Above that is Gia's dead face, her eyes open, her features frozen, a piece of hair pasted to her cheek with dried drool. Her chest isn't rising or falling.

Logan points the revolver at her head. "You finally did something good, something right," he says, tears welling, chills forming on his arms. "You knew if you didn't do it, I would." He wipes his eyes. "Didn't you!"

Although Logan has seen more dead animals than he can remember, having grown up on a farm and having to exterminate rodents and other thieves, this is only the second dead human he's ever seen. Keely's family believed that an open casket would allow her loved ones to have closure. Her embalmed remains, however, with overdone makeup, didn't look like her, and Logan resented them for doing that. Gia, on the other hand, looks just like herself. Logan takes his time looking her over.

Realizing he now has no reason to live, Logan begins to weep. He walks in a circle around the cabin, stopping at the window, looking out at the river. Although it's dark, he can just barely make out the black liquid flowing through the night.

He was baptized in a river at six or seven years old. His father had met a Christian woman, a woman who'd known Logan's mother, who had been at her funeral, a woman who was supposed to have been her friend but then goes and marries her widower. A handful of years later, she divorces him, the drunkard. Rage starts to brew.

The clouds part and reveal a sliver of moon, lighting the pistol in Logan's hand. He walks over to Gia and kneels with both knees on the floor, readying to pray. He takes off his headlamp and sets it down, the light still on.

He points the pistol at Gia's head.

"Lord," he says out loud. "I fear that you and the devil may be one and the same. I say this not to be defiant, but because you require honesty. On this night, Lord, I pray, and I beg, that you may forgive both the sinners in this cabin, two of your very own children, flawed as we may be, so flawed that we have committed the most egregious sin. We have killed, Lord, and we ask for your mercy. Please welcome us to your Kingdom. In your name, amen."

23

Through the woods, a gunshot cracks. Russ jumps up, panting, heart thumping. He sprints toward the cabin, navigating the darkness only by the tips of branches brushing his arms. Maybe it's a suicider, like the ones Cormac talked about. It can't be Gia—she doesn't have a gun, right?

Approaching the cabin, Russ leaps up the stairs and onto the porch, his momentum smashing him through the door. Gia is on the bed, her back against the wall, her lip trembling, her face ashen. On the floor beneath her, Logan Price is on his knees. Blood gushes from his chest, squirting and pooling onto a pistol and a small flashlight on the floorboards.

Russ goes cold. It's definitely Logan—but how?

Logan's head flops to the side, his eyes struggling to stay on Russ.

"Help me," he begs, wheezing, his hands pushing on his wound. "Please, I don't want to die. I made a mistake."

Russ looks at Gia and then at the gun. It's in Logan's reach.

Logan's head swivels slowly to Gia, his eyes squinting, his eyelids heavy.

"No," he says, whining, "no, it's not true, it can't be." His arms drop from his chest, his body swaying, his fingers dangling over the pistol. "I saw you—you were dead."

Gia trembles.

Russ steps toward Logan and the gun. "We're going to get you some help," he says.

"Why would God save *you*, Gia?" Logan asks, his jaw tightening. "Out of all the people he could have . . ." His fingers fumble for the gun. "You're the one who deserves His retribution."

As if lightning strikes his body, Logan's gaze freezes, and he gasps for air. He collapses, his head banging the bed frame, his bloody chest falling onto the gun. The muscles in his face loosen, his mouth and eyelids sticking half open.

The dawn sends morning light through the cabin's window, dust particles dancing in the light beams. The blood makes the room smell of iron.

Gia shivers, holding her wrist. "Is he dead?" she asks, her chin quivering. "Make sure he's dead."

Cautiously, Russ approaches Logan. He stops at the edge of the blood oozing out from underneath the body.

He lowers his hand to Logan's mouth, holding it there, feeling for his breath, but there's nothing. Russ pushes two fingers into Logan's neck. No pulse. "He's gone," he says, backing away.

"Are you sure?" She steps to the edge of the bed in Russ's direction. Struggling to balance, she begins to totter.

Russ hurries to her, carrying Gia off the bed and outside the door. Birds are chirping and singing and crowing. Gently, he sets her on the top step, leaning her back against the railing post. He takes her arm. "You're bleeding. Oh no, you're bleeding."

"I'm sorry," she says. "I'm so sorry."

"Stay here." Russ dashes back into the cabin, returning seconds later with the backpack. He grabs a clean sock and wraps it around the single cut made halfway across her wrist.

"There's a first aid kit in there," Gia says.

"In the bag?"

She nods.

"Of course."

With the care and focus of a paramedic, Russ rinses the wound, pats it dry, applies antiseptic, and closes it up with butterfly bandages. He helps her slide on a sweater, warming her and covering her bloodstained shirt.

She pulls her knees into her body and wraps her arms around her legs.

Russ sits next to her. "What happened?"

She rests her head on her lap, now sitting in an upright fetal position. "I found a nail," she says, sobbing but trying to control herself. "I was so angry. While I . . . used it, I had an episode. I guess my disease wants to be the one to finish me."

Russ scoots closer, placing his arm around her back.

She continues. "I woke to the gunshot. He was dazed, like he was possessed, not really here. Then you came in." She sobs into her pants. "I'm so sorry I asked you to leave."

Russ rubs her back. "Hey, you don't have to be sorry for anything."

They sit silently for a while, thinking about their next move. They've got to get out of here. There's a dead body in the cabin. Logan Price is dead.

Should they contact the authorities and explain what happened? Gia would be arrested for breaking parole, and she definitely wouldn't survive long in prison without a cure. However, if they don't report it, could they be charged? What if the cops think this was a murder? It is odd Logan shot himself in the chest and not the head.

"We need to go," Gia says, shaking. "Make sure we grab everything. We'll get down to Winnebago Flats and wait for a taxi to show up."

"I have Cormac's card," Russ says, digging into his pocket. "We can use Logan's phone."

"No, we can't do that. They'll look at his phone records. That call would put someone else here."

"But if he shot himself—"

"He did shoot himself," she snaps, "but we don't want the police deciding we might have had anything to do with this. I met people in prison who really were innocent. We need to go."

Russ stands. "Back to Seattle?"

She reaches her nonwounded arm up to Russ. "We have to at least get the Jeep back there. It can't be found in this area. Then, we'll figure it out."

Russ helps her up. "My mom won't be home yet. We can stay there. Her boyfriend hides money under the sink, in a fake dish soap bottle. We'll borrow it."

Russ goes back into the cabin to get any belongings still inside. He avoids looking at Logan's face. He grabs some clothes near the window. Then, on the bed, he finds the nail. He grabs it off the mattress.

As he's about to leave, Russ notices a familiar orange device sticking out of Logan's back pocket. Russ slides it out carefully.

———

While waiting for the water taxi at the dock, Russ scans through his messages and notifications. He recognizes that some of them have already been read. Logan had gotten into his phone, and Russ now realizes how Logan found them.

A bunch of the messages are about #RedButtRuss, but he pays them no attention. He finds a text from Morgan reminding him he needs to move out. The last notification is about Will's funeral. It's being held tomorrow, at the football field.

Russ clicks on his journal and writes.

My Journaling App - Entry #99:

The more I think about it, the more I realize that people are a lot like stars. They are born and then die. They shine for a time, and then turn into darkness, into space. But the darkness is not empty. It's something. We just don't fully understand what. So, I can't help but wonder: is all the space around us the same thing as the stars but just in a different form? Is it in some way . . . still alive? I hope so.

Russ pockets his phone, and the nail jabs him. Pinching it from his pocket, he stares at the tip, perhaps now mixed with both his and her blood. Gia holds out her hand. He meets her eyes for a moment. As he places the nail gently into her palm, she closes her fist around the metal and hucks it high and far into the water.

24

The ride back in the water taxi is quiet. Gia stays next to Russ. Cormac checks them in his rearview mirror several times, as if trying to decide if Gia wants to drive again. He doesn't ask.

The ferry is mostly empty, with the same captain but with less cheer. Perhaps he adopts a livelier demeanor for the trips to the dam with a larger crowd. They pass Kisser's Cove without a word from the captain, though one old couple kiss anyway.

Once they're driving back toward Seattle, Russ and Gia start to plan. They'll go to Russ's mom's apartment and stay for up to two nights, giving them a little time to organize. The money under the sink will help them get somewhere, although they won't get too far. Russ will attend the memorial while Gia waits at the apartment. Russ not going would look too weird—even weirder than him not being at the hospital when Will was in the ICU. More importantly, he wants to say goodbye to his friend. Gia, of course, can't risk being spotted, or she'll be in danger of going back to prison for ditching her ankle monitor, a clear violation of her parole. What's more, no one would want the Porta-Potty Pusher at the event.

At a rest stop, Russ sends a message to Tara to confirm her attendance at the funeral. He informs her that he'll bring the Jeep so she can return it to the lake house. When Tara asks about Gia, Russ tells her that he took her to her dad's, which is true; he just leaves out everything else. Although he'll no longer have the Jeep, he can walk back to the apartment from the memorial, since the event is being held down the street at the high school.

Where he and Gia will be going, and how they'll get there, they still don't know, but Russ has one person who might be able to help: J-Jack.

Mistaking J-Jack as just a janitor would be foolish. He spent significant time in the military, in a special forces unit. Although J-Jack would never speak of it, kids found pictures and articles of him receiving a prestigious military award. Hopefully, J-Jack can help in finding Gia's dad, who may be the only person who can save her at this point. It's a long shot, but it's Russ's only play, and besides, he could use some general advice from the only adult he can really trust.

As Russ takes the I-5 South onramp, and as farmland turns into city, his nerves start to rise. He is with a fugitive of sorts, her tracking monitor at the bottom of the Puget Sound, and they are heading back into the city where she is wanted. Additionally, he's now known in this area as Red-Butt Russ, something that he is not thrilled about, but which he has no choice but to accept, pretending it doesn't bother him, just as Will advised. Not only that, but his spanking is also all over the internet, and no matter what populous area he visits, he risks being exposed as the valedictorian who was lashed publicly by an old man. On top of it all, Russ will soon have nowhere to live.

Russ senses Gia's nervous energy as well. And why wouldn't she be nervous? She's the one who's wanted. More importantly, she needs a cure, and needs it fast, or she won't make it. Her failed suicide attempt seems to have given Gia some clarity: she wants to live. Her attitude has changed from one of resentment to one of urgency. How ironic that her disease, the source of her torment, is what saved her from ending her own life.

As Russ pulls the Jeep into the apartment complex, he looks around like a surveillance van might be waiting.

"Don't worry about someone looking for me," Gia says. "I'm not that big a fish. Like I said, they know that a huge percentage of those trackers will be removed. Besides, they probably hope I've already left Seattle, so they don't have to deal with me, the check-ins and all that."

Russ puts the Jeep in park. "You think we should tell someone about Logan or—"

"No," she snaps. "No way. Someone will find him, and they will know he shot himself. Admitting we were there only complicates things." She slides her finger across the GPS screen, deleting the trip history.

They enter the apartment. It's stale, quiet, and a little more dusty than usual. Russ turns on the shower. As he brushes his teeth, he hears the washing machine kick on in the room next to him. Gia is washing clothes. Russ smiles, then spits a wad of toothpaste mixed with grit into the sink.

After he dresses, he grabs a soda from the fridge. "Help yourself to anything," he says to Gia, who's lying on the couch watching the TV, a nature show. Ironically, or perhaps fittingly, the topic is crows. There are hundreds of them congregating around a dead bird. He pops open the can. "I shouldn't be too long. J-Jack lives about five blocks from here." He takes a swig, the burn of the carbonation cleansing the wilderness from his throat.

Russ has been to J-Jack's more times than he could remember. Usually, it was under the pretense that J-Jack had odd end jobs for Russ—mowing, weeding, etc.—wh ich Russ would have done for free, but for which J-Jack insisted he take a wage. Mostly, Russ spent his time there learning from the man, not completing tasks. They would sit in his backyard, and Russ would listen to him give advice about life. Although neither ever admitted it, J-Jack was the closest thing Russ ever had to having a dad.

Russ knocks on J-Jack's door. Through the doorbell cam, the man tells Russ to come in.

He goes straight to the back yard, the only place he's ever seen him sit. J-Jack is there, of course, and he rises from his seat. He's a tall, slender man with silver hair and muscles like a retired, but active, MMA fighter. As Russ extends his hand—a firm handshake being their customary greeting—J-Jack pulls him in for a hug. This takes Russ by surprise; the gesture warms him, even choking him up a bit.

"I'm sorry about Willie-B," J-Jack says. "I know how hard it is to lose a great friend."

Russ doesn't respond. If he does, he may lose it and cry in front of him.

On the wood-planked patio, two chairs face the Japanese garden–style backyard. Between the seats is an end table made from a stump, stained glossy and supporting a half-full glass of bourbon and an ash tray with an unlit cigar.

As they sit, J-Jack asks, "Where have you been? I tried calling a few times."

"I didn't have my phone for a couple days," Russ says.

"A teenager without a phone? I never heard of such a thing. Although, I guess you're not a teenager anymore." He lightly backslaps Russ's shoulder.

Russ grins and rubs his forearm. "With that graduation video out there, I'm not sure I'm glad to have the phone back."

"Ah, yes, the graduation speech. I wasn't going to bring that up, but what the hell was that all about?"

Russ leans over his knees and puts his head in his hands. "I keep telling myself that it doesn't matter compared to what happened to Will."

"Well, that's true. But it doesn't mean it doesn't matter at all."

Russ leans back in his chair. "I don't know what I was thinking."

"You were thinking about your high school crush. That's normal. What Eckspun did is as far from normal as you can get." J-Jack sips his whiskey. "I just know how hard you worked to get valedictorian."

Russ glances over at him.

J-Jack looks him in the eye. "At least Eckspun is done with," he says. "A forced retirement. Haha. And he has to eat some charges too. I know he thought his buddies at City Hall would get him off. Oh, you know what else, the school board is investigating those freaky administration parties thanks to your speech—and some old photographic evidence that came their way." J-Jack takes the unlit cigar from the ash tray. "Willie-B had your back though, getting up on that stage," he says, smiling with the cigar pinned between his lips. What a solid mother-fucker, right?"

Russ nods, chills rolling down his neck and arms.

"You know what," J-Jack says, lighting his stogie, "I keep thinking how odd it is that only Will was in that pool when the water became electrified. It was a pool party, and just one guy was in the water? What are the chances?"

"I don't think it was an accident," Russ says.

A puff of smoke exits J-Jack's lungs as he shifts his body toward Russ.

Russ takes a deep breath and says, "I think Logan did it. The guy is crazy crafty, I guess. He probably wired it up wrong or something. Plus, there's all that stuff that happened with Logan's girlfriend, the girl who died a few years back . . ."

"Keely Cristy. I knew her well—sweet kid. Gia Navarro freaking killed that girl."

"I think Keely got an infection."

"Doesn't matter." J-Jack presses his lips flat, his mus-tache taking their place. "Will and Keely were messing around, right? And Logan probably hated Will because of it."

"I'm not even sure if they were really messing around. Will never told me—"

"Doesn't matter. Perception drives action." J-Jack rolls his cigar with his fingers.

"There something else," Russ says. He considers telling J-Jack about the cabin but replays Gia's warning not to. "Will found a dead crow on his truck with its neck twisted around. He thought Logan did it."

"Hmmm," J-Jack says, rubbing the stubble on his chin. "That doesn't prove much."

Russ stands.

"Where you going?" The man leans back, over the arm rest.

Russ begins to pace. "I—I need your help with something."

J-Jack takes a long drag, the cherry glowing red. He nods.

"Gia is in my apartment."

He grins wide. "Ah," he says, "your recent absence is making a little more sense now."

"She's got this genetic disease—that's why they let her out. She needs to find her dad to see how he's survived with it so long, but she has no idea where he is."

"And you thought I would help with that?"

"I just thought—"

"I'm not sure I want to get mixed up in this. Gia Navarro pushed that girl into a literal shithole. What kind of a person does that? Young or not."

Russ examines the wooden porch. "I'm doing this for Will. I feel like I owe it to him."

J-Jack stubs out his cigar. "I'm sorry, Russ."

25

It's cool for June. As Russ approaches the school in the Jeep, people are getting out of cars wearing more school colors—puke-green clothing—than anything else. Cringe. Having the memorial at school is ridiculous, especially having it on the football field. Will didn't love football; he loved not to disappoint his dad. He didn't love this school either. He wanted to get out and break away.

Russ is wearing a short-sleeve button-down that grips his biceps, with three buttons undone, revealing the middle of his upper chest. This was Will's style, and wearing it is a simple way to pay homage. He backs the Jeep into Will's spot, in the same parking lot he drove out of after graduation with Russ hiding in the crew cab.

Russ walks up, keeping as much space as possible between him and others. He cuts through the outdoor hallways, through a maze of sidewalks, avoiding the main lane of people traffic. Even so, people have seen him, and he suspects at least someone has made a comment about Red-Butt Russ. Right now, however, he doesn't give a shit.

The stage has remained in place since graduation. How convenient. Russ walks around to the front of the stage. The white foldouts are in the same position, but there are no caps and gowns sitting in them. There are people of all sorts. On the front of the stage, two gigantic pictures of Will rest on stands, a family shot and a solo. In both, his smile is enormous, powerful, right to the dimples.

Russ scans the crowd for Tara, but he finds Big Jim Bayman instead. Jim is huge, built like a tank with love handles, which for some odd reason seem to make him even more attractive to women. Jim's back is turned, so he doesn't yet see Russ.

While looking at the photos of Will, Russ begins to imagine the pictures of himself that will be selected for his own funeral. The first one to pop into his mind is a picture he despises, freshman year, his face peppered with zits and his teeth covered with braces. As he continues to stare, the reality of the situation hits him: this is all that is left of Will; some pictures and stories.

As Russ approaches Will's dad, the people talking to him notice, prompting Jim to glance over his shoulder.

"Russ," Jim says, spinning around, opening his arms like an excited gorilla. "I'm glad to see you, boy."

"I'm so sorry, Jim."

Even though Russ is tall, his face still presses into Big Jim's chest as they embrace.

"You ain't got shit to be sorry for. It's not fair, Russ," Jim says, placing his giant hands onto Russ's shoulders. "I got your message, by the way. You are family, and I wish you could have been at the hospital. There were so many people. The staff made us ask almost everyone to leave. So, don't feel guilty about not being there. No one got to see him anyway, okay?"

Russ's eyes begin to tear up. He was focused on the craziness with Gia and Logan while everyone else was living the reality of Will's passing. It's not until this moment that Russ is truly experiencing the same.

Jim continues, "You were Will's best friend."

After someone dies, no words burn more deeply than "were" or "was. "

"Hey, another thing," says Big Jim, "It's a good thing I caught you before the event starts. Would you like to speak today? We are very restricted on how many people can speak, but if you want to, I'll put you on the list."

Without a thought about being back just days later, at a place where he embarrassed himself in front of another large crowd, Russ says, "Hell yes. It would be an honor."

Jim pats Russ on his shoulder. Their eyes are wet, but neither lets a tear fall.

"Pastor Vince will call you up," Jim says, clearing his throat.

Russ goes to the outside of the foldout seats, near the sideline, looking for a chair a few rows back, preferably by the aisle. Shortly after, he notices a hand waving him over from the middle of the third row. It's Tara, dressed in a dark brown jumpsuit, with her hair slicked back, exuding an appearance reminiscent of a Hollywood starlet. It seems rather ostentatious, somehow. Russ acknowledges her wave and carefully maneuvers toward her, sidestepping between the backs of chairs and knees, both bare and covered. Tara pats the empty seat beside her, while Rando and Sandra wave, sitting next to her on the other side.

As soon as he sits, Tara gently places her hand on his knee and kisses his cheek. Typically, Russ would blush, but this time he manages only a slight smile.

"You okay?" she asks, adopting a comforting tone.

"I'm good, I guess, considering the circumstances."

"Yeah, this is all so surreal."

There's a sea of heads around them, heads swaying and turning and crying.

"Hey," Tara says, in a quiet voice, "thank you for taking care of her."

Russ, and Tara it seems, would prefer that no one overhear anything about Gia, as Rando, Sandra, and others are seated nearby.

Lowering his voice to match hers, Russ says, "I'm glad she's alright." If he and Tara were somewhere more private right now, he would ask if her dad said anything about Logan at the lake house, but this isn't the time or the place.

As she surveys the heads around them, she asks, "Have you seen Logan?"

Damn. Logan is on her mind too. And it's weird she didn't call him Logy.

"Um, no, I haven't."

Rando's fist creeps over Sandra and then Tara. Russ looks down at it and then up at Rando, who's peering over his dark shades.

"Good to see you, Red," Rando says, smirking.

Sandra pushes his arm off her chest. "Oh, shut up," she says. "Hi, Russ."

Russ smiles at Sandra and fist-bumps Rando, sealing it with an up-nod.

People on stage ready the microphone, one tapping its head, the other yanking the cord. Russ waits for some kind of dirty joke from Rando, but he's busy whispering into Sandra's ear, making her giggle.

"How was LA?" Russ asks.

Tara tries to whip her slicked-back hair, but it doesn't move. "It was amazing, like discovering a new world. People are ambitious but fun. You should visit some-time."

"Yeah, sure. Maybe."

"Something's different about you," she says. "I like it."

Russ digs into his pocket and pulls out the key fob to the Jeep. "Thank you for lending this, and for the clothes and stuff."

He sets it in her open palm, the key fob clinking against her rings.

"Of course. Everything go okay?"

"Uh, yeah, pretty smooth. The Jeep is parked in Will's spot."

She smiles.

Audio feedback emanates from the stage. "Good morning, everyone. I am Pastor Vince, and I will be assisting with today's service." He's dressed in a full suit, and his shoes have a polished, military shine. "Will was loved by so many that we needed a big place," he says, spreading his arms wide to encompass the stadium. "After this, there will be a private funeral and burial for the family only, so we ask everyone to respect their privacy during that time." He covers the microphone as a young boy approaches, holding a piece of paper. The boy hands it to the pastor and hurries off stage.

"Before we commence sharing memories of the remarkable individual that Will was, I would like to express my gratitude to everyone for attending. Eventually, we will all leave this earth, and we can only hope to have impacted others as much as Will Bayman has impacted all of us." Pastor Vince unfolds the piece of paper. "Will's father, Jim, has organized several speakers for today's event. So many of you wanted to say something today, but our time is limited. So, please go to the website listed on the back of your programs should you like to post comments and stories about Will. Now, for our first speaker, Jim has asked that Will's best friend, Russ Burton, start us off."

Russ stiffens, his muscles rigid. He didn't expect to go first, but he rises, quickly, despite having no idea what he will say. As he shuffles back the way he came, he imagines people snickering about the pastor getting ready to swat that butt. Russ shakes it off. It's so insignificant, especially when considering why everyone is here. Will is gone forever. Now that's significant.

As he heads for the stage, the eyeballs follow him. Russ spots Mr. Huang near the stairs, a welcome sight. The teacher nods at Russ in encouragement. Passing the giant pictures, Russ stares at Will's blue eyes, so perfectly crafted, emanating gratitude. Five steps later, he's on the stage and approaching the same microphone that was the catalyst for the chaos at graduation.

Russ stands at the front of the stage, facing the crowd, each person there for different reasons—some to show their love for Will, some out of obligation, and others seeking a spectacle. Russ takes the microphone from the holder and takes one deep breath.

"There are so many people in this crowd, each living separate and unique lives."

Russ walks along the front of the stage.

"In moments like these, we join. Have you ever wondered why we do that? It may seem obvious, but it's not. It is true, as the pastor said, we are here to remember Will, but when we say that, what we really mean is that by remembering him, we show that Will's life mattered. And more than that, we want him to know that we love him."

Russ stops pacing at the center of the stage. He looks over the crowd.

"Let's do that right now, together. On three, let's join our voices and let him know, as loud as we can . . . We love you, Will. One, two, three . . ."

The crowd booms: "We love you, Will."

For a moment, Russ feels like a rockstar—fitting for the funeral of Will Bayman, a kind of rockstar in his own right.

Russ continues, "But that's not the only reason we are here."

The crowd settles.

"I learned recently that crows have funerals too. It's crazy. Hundreds of them will gather around a dead crow. Scientists believe the crows are trying to learn, figuring out what happened, how to move forward, and perhaps mourning one of their own. That makes sense to me. Aren't those some of the same reasons we are here today?

In the stands behind the field goal post, Russ notices a familiar sweatshirt. It's his Thrasher hoodie, a unique one with purple flames. He hasn't worn it since he was in Texas, when Glen the Great gave it to him while trying to get Russ to take up skateboarding, likely to get him out of Glen's space. Gia's face is shaded by the hoodie, her body shielded behind a group of tall spectators.

"Will was in this crowd just days ago, about to graduate. On that day, during what was perhaps the most humiliating moment of my life, Will came up on this stage right here, risking his own embarrassment, to stand next to me. We can all learn something from that."

Heads in the crowd nod along.

"Suddenly, Will's life is just over. It's so hard to accept that his story just came to an end like that when there was so much more to be written. During my speech that day, I spoke about the importance of making your story, as if our legacy is all that's left when where gone. But I never took the time to think about why I thought that was so important. Looking back, I think I had a false sense that if my story lived on, somehow so would I. But that's not true. Stories are important, but not for some immortality. Stories are important for the people we leave behind, because stories become the basis for what we do with our lives."

Russ pauses.

"Will's story is of someone who was loyal to his friends and who chose to be himself—authentic—over all else. He never acted as if he deserved anything because he didn't believe in . . . deservedness. What I mean is, he understood that the universe does not dole out rewards and punishments based on who deserves what. Life is about choices and action and everything else that follows, whether the outcomes make sense or not. With this . . . philosophy . . . Will rarely suffered. And maybe that's because suffering comes from the belief that we deserve more. This is part of Will's story that we can all take with us. And in doing so, we not only move forward with a better mindset, but we also move forward with Will, in a way, living on in all of us. Thank you."

The crowd rises, applauding instantly.

26

As Russ walks off the stage, people remain standing, clapping in unison. Out in front of the first row, Big Jim's paws smack the loudest, tears overspilling his eyelids, the liquid streaming to his quivering, rocklike chin. Russ holds eye contact until prickly chills ripple down his back.

Entering the green path running between the outer seats and the spectators along the sideline, Russ passes Mr. Huang, who tips his hat and grins. Instead of reentering the third row and rejoining Tara, Russ keeps walking. Tara, still clapping, glances around and squishes her manicured eyebrows together.

Aiming to get to Gia, but not wanting to reveal her presence, Russ pulls over to the sideline, taking an open spot between a young mom rolling a stroller back and forth and a middle-aged-woman shading her eyes with her palm. As he takes his position, both women look over and sandwich him with their smiles.

On stage, Pastor Vince takes the mic, and the crowd's attention resets onto the stage. Russ peers to the back of the stadium and finds Gia, her face tucked inside the hoodie like a turtle in its shell. He watches the pastor for a minute, waiting for the crowd to completely give their focus to him.

As Russ turns to go, a hand claps his shoulder.

"Mr. Burton," an authoritative voice says.

Russ turns slowly and the hand falls off his shoulder. In front of Russ is a man dressed in khakis and a white dress shirt, no tie, the sleeves rolled up.

The man sticks out a hairy-knuckled hand. "Detective Marcello, SPD," he says. "Can we talk for a moment?"

The middle-aged woman swallows hard, and the young mom tightens her grip on the stroller.

"Uh, yeah," Russ says.

As he follows the detective to a shady area next to an equipment shed, Russ makes sure not to even glance up at Gia.

"I thought you might be leaving," the detective says, "so I wanted to make sure we got to talk. But if you're not going, we can speak after the event."

"Wha . . . what's this about?" Russ asks, hoping Gia is seeing this and is already on the move.

"You sent us a message through our online reporting system."

The blood drains from Russ's face as the image of Logan's bloody body flashes in his mind. "I'm not sure . . . isn't that kind of thing anonymous?"

"Well, it can be Mr. Burton, but your submission included your name."

"How—"

"Where you signed in to any social media accounts? I ask because sometimes those will cause an autofill."

Russ rubs his forehead.

"I know this isn't an ideal time," Detective Marcello continues, "but we have reason to believe your concerns about Logan Price might be true."

Everything but the detective's cracked lips and gray mustache go black.

"You okay, Mr. Burton?" the lips say, the mustache bouncing above. The detective grips Russ's shoulder. "Why don't you take a seat."

Russ grabs the corner of the shed, bracing himself. "I'm okay, just give me a second."

"Of course, take your time."

What changed? Why would they now think Will's death was a homicide?

The rest of the detective's face comes into focus, and Russ's skin begins to cool with sweat, like a fever break.

"I know this is a lot to spring on you right now," Detective Marcello says, waiting for eye contact before continuing. "But Will's death is now an active homicide investigation."

A bead of sweat rolls down the back of Russ's right ear. "Will was right," he says.

The detective waits for more, his hands folded, resting on his cheap leather belt.

"The day he died," Russ says, "Will told me he was worried about Logan."

"Why would he be worried?"

Russ leans back against the shed. "They had history," Russ says, searching for a response that won't bring up Gia, "but Will never went into it."

"Will had dated Gia Navarro, right? The Porta-Potty Pusher. And that was Logan's girlfriend she pushed?"

Russ swallows and clears his throat. "I lived in Texas when all that happened, and Will never talked about it."

"Mr. Burton, I feel like you're not telling me something. You should know that Logan Price was found dead."

The pulse in Russ's neck thumps. "What?" He leans off the shed. "How did he die?"

"Apparently, it was a suicide."

"Oh my God."

"Mr. Price had a notebook in his pocket. It was somewhat of a journal."

Russ's neck beats harder.

"In it, Logan confesses to killing Will."

Russ's eyes widen.

"And he also mentions you."

"Me? Why—"

"He says you were helping Gia Navarro."

"What?"

"Mr. Burton, have you seen Ms. Navarro since her release from prison?"

Russ shakes his head. "I—"

"I need you to tell me the truth."

"No. I've never even met her."

The detective studies Russ's eyes. "Right. Well, I'd appreciate it if you didn't let Will's family know about this. I'm going to notify them after the funeral."

Russ nods. The detective pats him on the shoulder and turns to leave. After a few steps, he stops and turns around. "That was interesting what you said about crows. I didn't know that." He takes out a business card from his shirt pocket and hands it to Russ. "But I did know that they are one of the few animals that will hold a grudge. Crazy, right?"

The detective grins and walks away.

Russ takes a moment to get his breathing in rhythm. Logan confessed? The Bayman family will be devastated—their son's death was no accident, and to make matters worse, they allowed their son's killer inside the hospital while Will suffered in the ICU. And what about Gia? This is bad news for her. Once this gets out, the internet will reignite the story of the Porta-Potty Pusher, adding to it the revenge killing of Will Bayman. The state government will have to explain why Gia Navarro was released. And worse, they won't know her location, and the hunt will begin.

Russ stands on the sidelines again but closer to the rear bleachers. He fights the urge to look up for Gia until he's certain the detective can't see him. In the meantime, he watches Pastor Vince drone on.

Russ finally checks. Gia is gone. Pretending to take a call, he walks the perimeter, casually heading to the front. As he turns for the sidewalk leading away from the school, a familiar Toyota Tacoma pulls up. The window rolls down, revealing J-Jack wearing dark shades.

"You came," Russ says, lowering his phone. "I didn't think you would, seeing how you vowed never to step foot on these grounds again."

"I'm not so disgruntled that I wouldn't come back to say goodbye to my friend Willie-B. That was one good dude, and I'm glad I knew him."

"You leaving already?"

"I could ask you the same." J-Jack leans back. "For me, the first speaker said it perfectly. And once it's said . . . it's said."

Russ's eyes brighten and become glossy.

"Russ," J-Jack says, "I contacted an old friend. Doon Navarro wasn't hard to find. Apparently, a camper was able to get him a letter from Gia. He's in Seattle, look-ing for his daughter."

"What?" Russ leans in. "Where?"

"Mr. Navarro went to Gia's parole officer, looking for a way to contact her. But they arrested him on a warrant for drug manufacturing. Really, the guy was just making medicines for himself."

"No way. Which jail?" Russ asks, backing up as if ready to take off.

"I bailed him out, and I don't expect a refund. So, if he doesn't show for court, oh well. Consider it a gift to Willie-B."

Russ checks the back of the truck.

"He's with Gia," J-Jack says.

At that, Russ's stomach sinks. "They're gone?"

"They're waiting in the parking lot, in an old brown Dodge van."

Reaching through the window, Russ grips the re-tired janitor's thick forearm.

"You're welcome," he says.

Russ steps back, holding eye contact with his men-tor.

J-Jack shifts into drive. "Now, go make something of your scrawny self. I want to read about you in some publication, you hear, and not Barron's or some finan-cial bullshit like that. You got something special, Russ Burton."

The Tacoma pulls away. Russ stands tall, at attention, until the truck is gone.

He stuffs his phone into his pocket and hurries to the parking lot. At the entrance, he surveys the vehicles. The rusted van isn't hard to spot, and he jogs toward it.

"Russell," someone calls behind him.

He slows and turns to see Tara approaching, her hoop earrings swinging.

"Hey," she says, "where are you running off to?"

Russ chuckles. "I'm not exactly sure."

She wraps her arms around his torso and squeezes, pressing her face into his chest. "That was a great speech." She releases and locks on to his eyes. "You moved everyone."

"Thanks, I didn't even prepare anything."

She pokes his left pec. "It came from right here."

He smiles.

"But Russell, I was hoping you would come sit back down with me."

"Yeah, I got caught up talking with someone."

This is more focused attention than she's ever given him.

Tara studies his face. "So, I've been dying to know . . . how did everything go with Gia?"

Russ scratches the back of his neck. "Uh, you know, she's safe and sound."

"Did you two get to know each other pretty well?" She bumps her hip into his.

"Well enough, I guess."

"You know what," she says, placing her hand on his chest, "you should come with me to a party tonight. Some friends of mine at U-Dub invited me."

"Oh, I don't know. I'm not sure I feel up to it."

Hands on her hips, she says, "Oh, come on."

This must be weird for her. Tara usually can get a guy to do almost anything without much convincing.

"Actually," Russ says, "there's something I want to ask you about, too."

"Sure." She moves in closer.

"This is totally off topic, but . . . did Will really sleep with Keely?"

Her head snaps back. "I didn't see that coming. Why are you asking me that?"

"I just thought you might know."

Her face tightens, the stiffness matching her motionless, slicked-back hair. She looks back, perhaps hoping to see someone she knows so she can tell Russ to hold on, there's so-and-so, but no one is there. "I don't know for sure."

"Then why tell Gia they were hooking up?"

She folds her arms and looks behind again. "I guess I just had my suspicions, and I let her know."

Russ examines her eyes.

"You know what," Tara says, "I need to go—"

"I'm just going to come out and ask it. You were the one sleeping with Will, right?"

Her nostrils flare, and she steps into the space between them. "Everyone was sleeping with Will."

"Did you not want Gia to find out, so you threw shade on Keely?"

"What is this, huh? I invite you to hang out and you—"

"What if Keely was never with Will?"

"Everyone hooked up with Will," she says in a growl, her face an inch from his.

Russ just stares until Tara finally backs up.

"You know what, Russ, you're not who I thought you were." She stares at him, shaking her head. Then, she turns and storms off.

***

As Russ approaches the van, the rear door slides open. There's an empty seat, and Gia is sitting right next to it. Her hoodie is down, and her black hair splashes over the sweater.

"She didn't look too happy," Gia says.

Russ climbs in. "Oh, she wasn't."

"Doon Navarro," the driver says, reaching back to offer his hand. "Gia's dad."

"Nice to meet you, Mr. Navarro."

"Ha. None of that. Just call me Doon."

Doon is almost exactly how Russ pictured him: scruffy but handsome with a bald head.

"My dad has some good news," Gia says.

Russ looks at Doon.

"We're going to get my girl all fixed up. There's a place where cures are being discovered left and right. No bullshit."

He smells subtly of sweat.

Russ and Gia look at each other. She beams.

"We are heading north," Doon says, "far north. This place, man, it's wonderful, like nothing you've never seen. They do shit different, and they do it well, and live like humans should."

Doon reminds Russ of a Disney character, like a showman at a circus, but an honest one.

"They focus on spiritualism and science together," Doon says, interlacing his fingers, "as one. They'll change the world, Russ. They cured me one hundred percent. I haven't had an episode since."

"Sounds magical or something," Russ says.

"Yeah, it's something like that. The question that needs answering right now, man, is if you're coming with."

"Well, where is it exactly?" Russ asks.

"Yukon territory."

Russ smiles. "Back to Canada it is then."

Doon's grin reveals a surprising row of perfectly straight teeth.

"Excellent," he says, firing up the van. "They could use a smart, young guy like you—you're a valedictorian. That's what Mr. Jack told me."

Gia slides her fingers between Russ's.

"A place of science, huh?" Russ says. "Do they research the cosmos there?"

"Oh do they ever." Doon chuckles. "They got a goddamn observatory. How about that?"

In no time, the van is rumbling across the Puget. Gia's head rests on Russ's shoulder. From above, the water looks like a thick blue goo, oozing along, swirling as if it's mixing up the next batch of life. Russ's phone buzzes. It's Morgan. Without reading the message, he lowers the window. The air whooshes through the van. He flings the phone over the side of the bridge, watching it sail and fall forever out of view. Russ leaves the window down, the air whizzing around them. As he puts his arm around Gia, Doon punches the gas.

Dear Reader,

Thank you for picking up a copy of this novel. I truly hope you've enjoyed it. If you would like to share your thoughts about the characters, story, or anything else, I would love to hear from you. Feel free to email me, or if you want to leave a review on Amazon (or elsewhere), I read them. Lastly, if you're interested, I can send you more of Russ's journal entries. Just visit jakecayman.com and sign up. My email address is also there.

Until next time.

-Jake Cayman

www.ingramcontent.com/pod-product-compliance
Lightning Source LLC
Chambersburg PA
CBHW071511110726
47908CB00003B/797